PENGUIN BOOKS

Home Truths

David Lodge was born in London in 1935. He was educated at University College London, where he took his BA degree in 1955 and his MA in 1959. In between he did National Service in the British Army. He holds a doctorate from the University of Birmingham, where he taught in the English Department from 1960 until 1987, when he retired to become a full-time writer. He retains the title of Honorary Professor of Modern English Literature at Birmingham and continues to live in that city. He is a Fellow of the Royal Society of Literature and was made a CBE for services to literature in the 1998 New Year Honours List.

David Lodge's novels include *The Picturegoers* (1960); *Ginger, You're Barmy* (1962); *The British Museum is Falling Down* (1965); *Out of the Shelter* (1970); *Changing Places* (1975), for which he was awarded both the Hawthornden Prize and the *Yorkshire Post* Fiction Prize; *How Far Can You Go?*, which was Whitbread Book of the Year in 1980; *Small World*, which was shortlisted for the Booker Prize in 1984; *Nice Work*, which won the 1988 *Sunday Express* Book of the Year Award and was also shortlisted for the Booker Prize; *Paradise News* (1991); and *Therapy*, regional winner and finalist for the 1996 Commonwealth Writers Prize. He has written several books on literary criticism, including *Language of Fiction* (1966), *The Novelist at the Crossroads* (1971), *The Modes of Modern Writing* (1977), *Working with Structuralism* (1981), *Modern Criticism and Theory* (editor, 1988) and *After Bakhtin: Essays on Fiction and Criticism* (1990). In addition, he has published *Write On* (1986), a selection of occasional essays; *The Art of Fiction* (1992), a collection of articles which originally appeared in the *Independent on Sunday*; and

The Practice of Writing (1996), an entertaining collection of essays, lectures, reviews and a diary on various aspects of creative writing. His work has been translated into more than twenty languages and many of his books are available in Penguin.

Small World was adapted as a television serial in 1988 and he himself adapted *Nice Work*, which won the Royal Television Society's Award for the best drama serial of 1989 and a Silver Nymph at the International Television Festival in Monte Carlo in 1990. In 1994 he adapted *Martin Chuzzlewit* for a six-part BBC television serial. His first stage play, *The Writing Game*, was produced at the Birmingham Repertory Theatre in 1990, and he adapted it for Channel 4 TV in 1995.

Home Truths

A Novella

D A V I D   L O D G E

PENGUIN BOOKS

PENGUIN BOOKS

Published by the Penguin Group
Penguin Books Ltd, 27 Wrights Lane, London w8 5tz, England
Penguin Putnam Inc., 375 Hudson Street, New York, New York 10014, USA
Penguin Books Australia Ltd, Ringwood, Victoria, Australia
Penguin Books Canada Ltd, 10 Alcorn Avenue, Toronto, Ontario, Canada m4v 3b2
Penguin Books (NZ) Ltd, Private Bag 102902, NSMC, Auckland, New Zealand

Penguin Books Ltd, Registered Offices: Harmondsworth, Middlesex, England

First published in Great Britain by Secker & Warburg 1999
Published with an Afterword in Penguin Books 2000

2

Set in 11.75/15.5 pt Monotype Garamond
Phototypest by Intype London Ltd
Printed in England by Clays Ltd, St Ives plc

Author's Note

This novella is based on my play of the same title, which was first produced at the Birmingham Repertory Theatre in February 1998, and subsequently published as a playtext by Secker & Warburg. I have revised some of the dialogue, restored lines that were cut from the play for various reasons at various stages of its composition, changed a few details, and added some new material. But it is essentially the same story.

DL

To Leah

'**home truth:** a wounding mention of a person's weakness'

Shorter Oxford English Dictionary

I

The cottage stands all on its own at the end of a rutted cart-track that leads off from the main road to the village, about a mile away. It is easy to drive past this gap in the hedgerows without seeing the small hand-painted wooden sign, faded and weathered, which is nailed to a post, bearing the name 'Ludlow'; and without realizing therefore that it leads to a human habitation. A slight hump in the terrain and a stand of beech trees screen the cottage and its outbuildings from the road.

This is not one of the more picturesque parts of Sussex, but a little pocket of slightly scruffy agricultural land situated between the main roads from London to Brighton and Worthing. Gatwick airport is nearer than the South Downs. The cottage itself is quite old, but not architecturally distinguished. It looks as if it originally consisted of two small semi-detached cottages, probably occupied by farm-workers, which have been converted into a single dwelling in modern times with many improvements and modifications.

The front door is actually on one side of the house, where a gravel drive has been laid out for car parking, and the long frontage has windows where there were once doors, overlooking a pleasant, unpretentious garden of lawn and shrubs and flower-beds. At the back a one-storey extension has been added, accommodating a modern kitchen and a white-tiled shower suite. There are other outbuildings, including a kind of lean-to providing shelter for a small kiln, and what looks at first sight like a garden shed, except that it is constructed of rather superior wood and has only one small square window, set into the door and glazed with dark, opaque glass.

'Did you know', said Adrian, reading from the carton, 'that cornflakes are eighty-four per cent carbohydrates, of which eight per cent are sugars?'

Eleanor, absorbed in her newspaper, did not answer. Adrian picked up another packet and scrutinized it.

'All-Bran is only forty-six per cent carbohydrates, but eighteen per cent of them are sugars,' he said. 'Is eighteen per cent of forty-six better or worse than eight per cent of eighty-four?'

Eleanor still did not answer. Adrian did not seem surprised or offended. He picked up another packet.

'Shredded Wheat seems to be the best bet. Sixty-seven per cent carbohydrates, of which less than one per cent are sugars. And no salt. I suppose that's why it doesn't taste of anything much.' He put a portion of Shredded Wheat into his bowl, and poured on semi-skimmed milk.

It was nine o'clock on a Sunday morning in the summer of 1997. Adrian and Eleanor Ludlow were in the living room of their cottage, in dressing gowns. It was a large, low-ceilinged, comfortable room, with a dining table at one end and a sitting area at the other, where there was an open fireplace. The walls were lined with densely packed bookshelves, which seemed to lean inwards in places – an effect of the irregularity of the walls, which made the house seem like a rather civilized cave dwelling. Spaces had been left in the shelving for the display of several ceramic vases, jugs and bowls with a family resemblance in their design; and there were more such objects on occasional tables in the room. The bookshelves also incorporated an expensive hi-fi system, which was silent at this hour, like the television set pushed into a corner of the sitting area. Adrian was at the dining table. Eleanor had finished her breakfast and was sitting on the sofa reading the Sunday papers. She did this systematically. On one side of her was a neat stack of pristine, folded, multi-sectioned broadsheets; on the other a less tidy pile of the sections she had finished with. She wore a pair of cotton gloves to stop the ink of the newsprint from soiling her hands and getting on her clothes.

'A new British film is causing a stir in America,' she said. She was reading the Culture section of the *Sunday Gazette*. 'It's about male strippers in Sheffield.'

'I suppose that might have some perverse exotic attraction for Americans,' said Adrian. 'I can't see it catching on here. What else is new in the world of artistic endeavour?'

Eleanor scanned the pages of the newspaper. 'Damien Hirst is exhibiting a decapitated art critic in a tank of formaldehyde,' she said, then quickly corrected herself: 'Oh no, that's a joke.'

'It's so hard to tell the difference these days,' said Adrian.

'And there's a row brewing over the Royal Opera House.'

'It all sounds reassuringly familiar,' said Adrian.

A jet passed overhead. The cottage was about twelve miles from Gatwick airport and under its main flight path. The noise sometimes disturbed visitors, but Adrian and Eleanor scarcely noticed it any longer.

'What's the front-page news?' Adrian asked.

Eleanor put down the *Gazette* and picked up the news section of the *Sunday Sentinel*.

'Boring,' she said. 'Mostly about Diana's holiday with Dodi Fayed.'

'But it was *last* Sunday, too!' said Adrian.

'It's the ultimate silly season story,' said Eleanor. 'One of the tabloids has paid a quarter of a million for pictures of them kissing on his yacht.'

'You could get quite a good Picasso for that,' said Adrian. 'A small one, anyway.'

Eleanor's eyes widened as she glanced at the foot of the page. 'Good God!' she exclaimed.

'What's the matter?'

'I don't believe it.' She dropped the news section and began to search through the pile of unread sections of the *Sentinel*.

'What has happened to cause this amazement he asked himself,' said Adrian, who had once been a novelist by occupation. 'Has Jeffrey Archer renounced his peerage? Has Richard Branson travelled on one of his own trains? Has –'

'It says there's an interview with Sam in the *Sentinel* Review,' said Eleanor. 'By Fanny Tarrant.'

'Oh, yes,' said Adrian.

Eleanor looked up in surprise. 'You knew about it?'

'Well, sort of. The Tarrant woman called me up about it.'

'You didn't tell me.'

'I forgot,' said Adrian. 'You were out, I think.'

'What did she want?'

'Background about Sam,' said Adrian.

'I hope you didn't give her any.'

'I told her I wouldn't discuss my oldest friend behind his back.'

'I should think not,' said Eleanor. She found the *Sentinel* Review and pulled it from the pile. 'Especially with Fanny Tarrant. She eats men like Sam for breakfast.'

Adrian looked at a spoonful of Shredded Wheat halfway to his mouth. 'Well, there's not a lot of sugar in Sam,' he said.

'Sir Robert Digby-Sisson wept when he read what Fanny Tarrant wrote about him,' said Eleanor, turning the pages of the Review.

'How do you know?' said Adrian.

'It said so in another paper. Here it is. God, what a ridiculous photograph. I fear the worst. Look!' Eleanor held open the paper for Adrian to see the large colour photograph of Sam Sharp. 'He's wearing riding boots. He doesn't ride. He doesn't even own a horse.'

'They're not riding boots, they're cowboy boots,' said Adrian. 'He wears them on his trail bike.'

'Trail bike! When is he going to grow up? Anyway, he isn't on a motorbike in the picture, he's sitting in front of his computer, and a right wally he looks too, in cowboy boots . . . Oh dear. Oh dear. Listen to this.' Eleanor began to read the article aloud. '"*Samuel Sharp has done pretty well for the son of a tobacconist in darkest Deptford. He owns a modernized seventeenth-century moated farmhouse in Sussex with its own tennis court, and a hundred and fifty acres of arable land which he leases to neighbouring farmers because he's too busy writing lucrative TV screenplays to farm them himself. You can tell that he fancies himself in the agrarian role, though, by the way he swaggers around his estate with his Ralph Lauren jeans tucked into high-heeled cowboy boots. He can use the heels, actually, being a little short in the shank. Stature is a sensitive point with him. 'Whatever you do, don't ask Sam about his height,' said a friend. 'Or his toupée.' I didn't know till then that he wore a toupée.*" Some friend!' said Eleanor. And then: 'Was that you?'

'Certainly not,' said Adrian. 'Where's the low-sugar marmalade?'

'We've run out.' Adrian tutted. Eleanor continued reading aloud from the newspaper. '"*Naturally these no-go areas only excited my curiosity. I spent much of our time together on tiptoe, trying to inspect the top of Samuel Sharp's*

7

head for tell-tale signs of his rug. When he saw what I was doing he would rise up on his toes to frustrate me, so we must have looked like a couple of ballet dancers doing warm-up exercises. Except that there was nobody there to see us. Mrs Sharp left the ranch three months ago. Rumour has it that she has moved in with the director of her husband's last TV series, the BAFTA-winning The Bottom Line. *Samuel Sharp was rather tight-lipped about this when I raised the subject. 'Laura and I separated by mutual agreement,' he said. Laura, incidentally, was wife number two, number one having departed some years ago, taking their two children with her . . ."* What business is that of hers? Or anybody else's?' Eleanor commented, and went on reading aloud.

'"*The first thing you notice about Samuel Sharp's study is that it's plastered with trophies, certificates and citations for prizes and awards, and framed press photographs of Samuel Sharp, like the interior of an Italian restaurant. The second thing you notice is the full-length mirror on one wall. 'It's to give the room a feeling of space,' the writer explained, but you can't help thinking there's another reason. His eyes keep sliding sideways, drawn irresistibly by this mirror even while he's speaking to you. I went to see Samuel Sharp wondering why he had been so unlucky in matrimony. I left thinking I knew the answer: the man's insufferable vanity.*"'

Eleanor looked at Adrian for a reaction. He was spreading marmalade thinly on a piece of cold toast.

'A bit harsh,' said Adrian.

'Harsh! It's vicious,' said Eleanor. She continued reading silently to herself for a few moments, with little sighs of dismay and stifled sniggers, then broke into speech again. 'Oh God, listen to this. "*The heroine of Samuel Sharp's latest TV film,* Darkness, *is described in the BBC's publicity handout as a 'nymphomaniac'. I asked him if he had ever met a nymphomaniac. 'Yes, no, well, it depends on what you mean by a nymphomaniac,' he stammered. 'I've known women who made it pretty obvious that they'd, you know, if I gave them the slightest encouragement, but it's difficult to say whether it was nymphomania, exactly . . .' I think he was delicately hinting that it's difficult for a handsome chap like him to know whether the readiness of casual female acquaintances to roll over on to their backs and open their knees is the effect of their temperament or his irresistible sex appeal.*"' Eleanor laid down the newspaper. 'Sam's going to be devastated when he sees this,' she said.

'Well, he did ask for it, one might say,' said Adrian.

'You're not very sympathetic to your best friend,' said Eleanor.

'I said "oldest friend".'

'Who's your best friend, then?'

Adrian thought for a moment. 'You are.'

Eleanor was unmoved by this declaration. 'Apart from me.'

'I don't think I've got one,' he said. 'Sadly, it's not a concept that belongs to middle age.'

Adrian had celebrated his fiftieth birthday earlier in the year. Eleanor was a couple of years younger. Some thirty years ago they had been students together with Sam Sharp at a provincial university. They had both aged gracefully. Adrian was tall and slim, slightly stooped, with a mane of silver-grey hair worn long over his ears and neck. Eleanor was still a good-looking woman, pleasant to behold even at this hour of the morning, before she had washed and attended to her appearance. A cloudy mass of fine wavy hair, discreetly coloured, framed a round, well-fleshed face with big brown eyes and a generous mouth and chin. She had kept her teeth and her figure.

At that moment they heard the sound of a car turning into the gravel drive outside the cottage.

'Who can that be?' said Eleanor.

Adrian went to the window and looked out, squinting sideways at the parking space. 'It's Sam,' he said.

'Hah, hah,' said Eleanor calmly. She resumed reading Fanny Tarrant's interview.

'Is he not the owner of a green Range Rover, registration number SAM 1?' Adrian inquired.

Eleanor jumped to her feet, and went to the window

to look out. 'My God, it *is* Sam,' she said. She hurried towards the door, stopped, turned back and thrust the *Sentinel* Review into Adrian's hands. 'Here, hide this,' she said.

'Why?' said Adrian. The doorbell chimed.

'He may not have seen it yet.'

'Where?'

'Anywhere.'

The doorbell chimed again and Eleanor hastened out to the hall, stripping off her cotton gloves and stuffing them into the pockets of her dressing gown. Adrian heard her unbolting the front door, then opening it, crying with an effect of surprise, 'Sam! What are you doing here at this time of the morning? Come in.' Adrian slid the *Sentinel* Review under a cushion on the sofa. Then, as an afterthought, he thrust all the other newspapers under the sofa, out of sight, just as Eleanor returned with Sam. 'Adrian, look who it is,' she said.

''Allo, mate,' said Sam. The more successful he had become, the more he favoured the accent of his Cockney roots. But his greeting lacked real warmth and his smile was restrained, like those exchanged between friends at funerals. He was holding a furled newspaper in one hand, and tapped it against his upper thigh. He was dressed in clean, well-pressed jeans, an unstructured suede jacket and a cotton polo shirt, each of which bore the name of a different well-known designer. Sam was not as short as Fanny Tarrant had implied, but slightly less than average in height. His complexion was tanned and wrinkled with laugh-lines around the eyes, his features slightly monkey-like, with a snub nose and a deep upper lip.

'Sam!' said Adrian, weakly imitating Eleanor's tone of surprise. 'What brings you here so early on a Sunday morning?' He advanced with hand outstretched. To shake it, Sam had to transfer the newspaper from his right hand to his left. It was a copy of the *Sentinel* Review.

'I'm flying to LA this morning, from Gatwick,' Sam said. 'Thought I'd drop in on my way.'

'What a lovely surprise,' said Eleanor. 'We haven't seen you for ages. Have you had breakfast?'

'As much as I could stomach,' said Sam.

'Would you like some coffee?'

'Thanks, that would be nice.'

'I'll make some fresh.' Eleanor picked up the coffee pot.

'No, don't bother,' said Sam. 'That will do fine. I like lukewarm coffee.' He held up the *Sentinel* Review. 'Have you seen this?'

'What is it?' said Eleanor.

'Today's *Sentinel*. Did you read what that bitch Fanny Tarrant has written about me?' He sat down on the sofa, sensed the presence of the newspaper underneath the cushion, and pulled it out. 'I see you have,' he said.

'I just glanced at it,' said Eleanor.

'Did *you*?' Sam asked Adrian.

'Ellie read out some bits to me,' he said. Sam looked reproachfully at Eleanor.

She handed him a cup of coffee. 'Only the beginning.'

'Well, it doesn't get any better,' said Sam.

'How do you feel about it?' said Adrian.

'I feel as if I've been shat on from a great height by a bilious bird of prey,' said Sam.

Adrian smiled. 'That's rather good. Did you just think of it?'

'It's a quotation,' said Sam.

'Is it?' said Adrian. 'From what?'

'From my last series but one.'

'Sam,' said Eleanor, 'what possessed you, to let that woman interview you? You must have read her stuff.'

'I suppose so . . . I can't remember,' said Sam. 'There are so many of them, with their columns and their interviews . . .'

'But she's famous,' said Eleanor.

13

'No, *I'm* famous,' said Sam, placing his index finger on his chest. 'She hasn't been around long enough to be famous.'

'Notorious, then. For being rude about people.'

'Well, she rang me up one day, drooling over *The Bottom Line*. She really seemed to love it.'

'And you fell for that old ploy?' said Eleanor.

'I know, I know . . . But I just didn't think that someone who could say such intelligent things about my work would write anything so . . .' Sam shook his head in disbelief at the perfidy of Fanny Tarrant. 'I gave her lunch, too. Prepared it myself: home-made watercress soup, cold poached salmon with mayonnaise – real mayonnaise, not that stuff like Brylcreem out of a jar. And a bottle of Pouilly-Fuissé that cost a hundred and fifty quid a case.'

'Poor Sam,' said Eleanor.

'It does seem ungrateful,' said Adrian. 'After the mayonnaise and everything.'

'I suppose you think it's funny?' said Sam.

'No, no,' said Adrian. Sam stared at him suspiciously. 'No,' Adrian repeated, shaking his head vigorously. But his lips twitched.

'I'm going to throw some clothes on,' said Eleanor. 'You can stay a little while, Sam?'

'Half an hour or so.'

'Oh good. I won't be a minute. We haven't seen you for ages.'

'No, I've been insanely busy lately. I haven't seen anyone,' said Sam.

'Except Fanny Tarrant,' said Adrian, as Eleanor left the room.

'That was work,' said Sam. 'Just because you've backed out of the limelight, Adrian, you needn't feel superior to those of us who still have to hang in there.'

'*Hang in there* . . .? I'm afraid your speech is being corrupted by all these meetings in Hollywood, Sam.'

'I've got a particularly important one on Tuesday. I hope to God they don't take the *Sunday Schadenfreude* at the studio.'

'You can be sure someone will send it to them.'

'Thanks for cheering me up.'

'It's the world we live in, Sam. Or, rather, the world *you* live in.'

'What world is that?'

'A world dominated by the media. The culture of gossip.'

'The culture of envy, you mean,' said Sam. 'There are people in this country who simply hate success. If you work hard, make a name, make some money, they'll do everything in their power to do you down.'

'But you put yourself in their power by agreeing to

be interviewed by the likes of Fanny Tarrant,' Adrian said.

'It's easy to say that when you've never been asked.'

'I have been asked,' said Adrian.

Sam looked at him in surprise. 'What, by Fanny Tarrant? When?'

'A few weeks ago.'

'And what did you say?'

'I said "No, thanks."'

'Why did she want to interview you?'

'I'm not a completely forgotten writer, you know,' said Adrian.

'Of course not. I didn't mean . . .' Sam floundered for a moment.

'*The Hideaway* is a set text at "A" Level.'

'And so it should be,' said Sam, recovering his poise. 'But *The Hideaway* was published nearly twenty years ago. Sunday papers usually go for something a little more topical. What was Fanny Tarrant's hook?'

'Hook?'

'Yes, hook. For example,' Sam said, as if explaining something to a child, '*my* interview is hooked to the upcoming transmission of *Darkness*.'

'Oh, got you.'

'But I doubt if Fanny Tarrant was proposing to hang her interview with you on the *Paragon Book of*

Cricket Writing. That was your most recent anthology, wasn't it?'

'No, it was *Wills and Testaments*, actually,' said Adrian. 'I really don't know why she wanted to interview me. It was just an aside. She actually called to ask me some questions about *you* . . .'

'I hope you didn't tell her anything.'

'Of course not.'

'Well, somebody did. Somebody told her that I . . .' Sam left the sentence incomplete.

'Wear a toupée?' Adrian said. Then, as Sam looked accusingly at him: 'It wasn't me!'

Sam seemed to believe him. 'If I could get my hands on her now, I'd strangle the bitch,' he said.

'Why allow yourself to get so angry?' said Adrian. 'That's exactly what she wants. Deny her the satisfaction. Laugh it off.'

'You wouldn't say that if you'd read the whole thing.'

'Let's have a look,' said Adrian. He took the paper from Sam, found the relevant page, and began to read silently. After a few moments he gave a snuffling laugh. 'She's quite witty, isn't she?' he said.

'Do you think so?' said Sam coldly.

'What's she like?' Adrian asked, continuing to read.

'Fanciable but frigid. Good legs. I never got a proper look at her tits, she kept her jacket on.'

Adrian looked up from the page and sighed. 'I meant, what social type?'

'Oh . . .' Sam thought for a moment. 'Essex girl with attitude. She went to Basildon Comprehensive and read English at Cambridge. Calls herself a post-feminist.'

'So she does,' said Adrian. He read aloud from the newspaper: '"*Samuel Sharp said, 'I never did understand that word.' I said it meant that I'd assimilated feminism without being obsessed by it. He said, with a roguish smile, 'Oh, then I'm a post-feminist too.' I said that the treatment of women in his screenplays made that hard to believe. He bridled somewhat: 'What do you mean?' I explained that I'd been looking at videos of all his TV films and series, and without exception they all featured scenes in which women were naked and men were clothed. The striptease joint in* The Bottom Line, *the artist's studio in* Brush Stroke, *the operating theatre in* Fever Chart, *the Peeping Tom scene in* Happy Returns, *the rape scene in* Shooting the Rapids, *the slave market scene in* Dr Livingstone, I Presume . . ."' Adrian glanced at Sam, who was growing restive at this recital. 'She certainly did her homework, didn't she?'

'She's picking out one tiny component of my work and blowing it up out of all proportion,' said

Sam. 'Every one of those scenes is justified in context.'

Adrian continued reading aloud: '"*And in his latest film,* Darkness*, which he directed himself*" – Is that wise, directing yourself?'

'Who understands my work better?'

Adrian stared at Sam for a moment, as if lost for words, then resumed: '"*And in his latest film,* Darkness*, which he directed himself, there's a long scene in which a young woman walks around her apartment naked, preparing a meal for a man who's fully clothed.*"'

'But that's because she thinks he's blind!' said Sam.

'"*But that's because she thinks he's blind!' Samuel Sharp exclaimed,*"' said Adrian, reading from the newspaper. '"*As if that made it all right. I said, 'But we know he* isn't *blind. Doesn't that just intensify the voyeuristic thrill? Isn't it the schoolboy fantasy of being invisible in the girls' locker room?' Samuel Sharp's eyes had now begun to flicker sideways towards the wall mirror at a quite alarming rate.*"'

'You get the picture,' said Sam. 'It's a hatchet job.' He held out his hand for the newspaper, but Adrian carried on reading aloud. He seemed to be enjoying himself.

'"*I said I'd heard that he had made a fuss about being excluded from the closed set for the rape scene in* Shooting the Rapids. *He said it was the actress who had made all the*'

*fuss, as if nobody had ever seen her without her knickers before.
I asked him how he would feel about having his knickers ripped
off in front of a small circle of silent, intent men wielding bits
of machinery. He said, 'Actors may have to bare their bums
occasionally. I bare my soul every time I put finger to keyboard.'"*
Adrian stopped reading and looked at Sam. 'Did you
really say that? "*I bare my soul every time I put finger to
keyboard*"?'

'Possibly,' said Sam, a shade defensively. 'But the
rest is a tissue of lies and distortions. I'm going to
write a letter to the paper.'

'Write it, by all means, but don't post it,' said Adrian,
putting down the newspaper.

'Why not?'

'You'll only make yourself look weak.'

'Well, I've got to do something.'

For some moments both men gave silent thought
to this matter. 'You could put Fanny Tarrant into your
next television series, thinly disguised as a raving
nymphomaniac,' Adrian suggested.

Sam shook his head. 'I've thought of that. It would
never get past the lawyers.'

'You'll just have to grin and bear it, then.'

Sam looked at Adrian. 'It would be more effective
if the counter-attack came from somebody else . . .'

'Oh no,' said Adrian.

'What?'

'You want *me* to write a letter to the *Sentinel*?'

'No, I've got a better idea,' said Sam. 'Suppose you agree to be interviewed by Fanny Tarrant . . .'

'Sounds like a very bad idea to me,' said Adrian.

'No, listen . . . Remember how we hoaxed that reporter from the local rag in 'sixty-eight? During the great sit-in?'

Adrian smiled. 'How could I forget?' He raised his fist and recited: '"*The Student Revolutionary Council demands appointment of professors by democratically elected committees representing all sections of the university.*"'

'"*Including porters, tea-ladies and cleaning staff,*"' said Sam. 'Don't forget them.'

'"*We demand student self-assessment instead of exams.*"'

'"*Double beds for students cohabiting in University residences.*"'

'"*Smoking of marijuana to be permitted in tutorials.*"'

'And he wrote it all down like a lamb and went away and they printed it all over the front page of the *Post.*'

They laughed reminiscently together, until the penny dropped for Adrian. 'You're not suggesting that I try to hoax Fanny Tarrant?' he said.

'Why not?'

'Pretend to be a wife-beating paedophile drug

addict, you mean? And hope she'd be silly enough to print it?'

'Well, it needn't be quite as lurid as that,' said Sam.

Adrian shook his head. 'This woman isn't a provincial cub reporter, Sam. It wouldn't work.'

'No, you're probably right,' Sam said regretfully. He frowned and grimaced with concentrated thought. Then, 'Hang about!' he said. His countenance cleared. '*Hang about!* Suppose you give her a straight interview, but use the opportunity to write a piss-take profile of *her*, for one of the other papers?'

'What?' said Adrian.

'Remember those satirical character sketches you used to write for the old mag? "The Clap-Happy Chaplain", "The Vicious Vice-Chancellor". You could do something on those lines.'

'"The Invidious Interviewer"?'

'That's the idea. As long as it's absolutely obvious who it's about, we wouldn't have any trouble placing it. There are lots of people who would like to see Fanny Tarrant taken down a peg or two. I know someone on the *Chronicle* who'd jump at it.'

'No doubt, Sam, but –'

Sam hopped around the room, consumed with the beauty of his conception. 'Turn the tables on the bitch! Interview her when she thinks she's interviewing you!

Dig into her background. Find out what makes her tick. Why the envy? Why the malice? Lay it all out. Give some of her own medicine. Wouldn't that be brilliant?'

'You don't think she'd be suspicious if I rang her up and said I'd changed my mind?'

'Nah. You've no idea how arrogant these people are. They think the whole world is just longing to be interviewed by them.'

'That wasn't the impression I gave her the other day,' said Adrian.

'Then we'll get someone else to ring her up for you . . .' Sam said. 'Your agent! The perfect alibi: you mentioned her invitation casually to him and he talked you into doing it.'

'Well, of course Geoffrey would love to see my name in the papers again, but –'

'There you are!' cried Sam. 'You could do a wonderful piece, Adrian. Weave in all that stuff about the culture of gossip. You'd enjoy it.'

'There's just one drawback to your scheme.'

'What's that?' said Sam.

'I'd get stitched up by Fanny Tarrant in the process.'

Sam was silenced for a moment. 'Not necessarily,' he said at length.

'No?'

'No . . . She isn't always bitchy.'

'I thought you couldn't remember whether you'd read her stuff.'

'I saw a nice piece by her once, about somebody. Who was it?' He frowned as he tried to remember.

'Mother Teresa?' Adrian inquired facetiously.

'God, no, she was vicious about Mother Teresa,' said Sam.

'Mother Teresa gave her an interview?' Adrian asked incredulously.

'No, it was one of her diary columns . . . Fanny Tarrant can't bear the thought of somebody being both genuinely good and seriously famous.'

'Well, that would leave me in the clear, certainly,' said Adrian.

'Look,' said Sam earnestly. 'These people dare not write knocking copy *all* the time, otherwise nobody would ever speak to them. Every now and again they do a sympathetic interview just to keep the pot boiling. I bet she's got you lined up as her next Mr Nice Guy.'

'Did you hope to fill that slot yourself?' said Adrian.

To judge from Sam's expression, this was a shrewd guess. 'Come on, Adrian,' he said cajolingly, 'I'm your old mate. Do this for me. Please!' And he went down theatrically on his knees.

Eleanor, now dressed in a loose cotton frock, came

into the room. 'What's going on?' she said, smiling.

'Sam wants to take out a contract on Fanny Tarrant, with me as the hit man,' Adrian explained.

Sam scrambled to his feet. 'Well, when Adrian told me that she's itching to interview him –' he began.

Eleanor stared at Adrian. 'Fanny Tarrant wants to interview *you*?'

'She mentioned it when she rang me up about Sam.'

'The idea is –' said Sam.

'But why?' Eleanor's attention was still focused on Adrian.

'I don't know. She was probably just buttering me up.'

'The idea is, you see –'

'*Sam's* idea is –' Adrian interjected.

'The idea is', said Sam, 'Adrian agrees to be interviewed in order to write a satirical profile of Fanny Tarrant – without her knowing, of course.' Eleanor continued to stare at Adrian, as Sam babbled on, rubbing his hands together. 'I like it the more I think about it. It could be the start of a whole new genre. The worms turn. The artists fight back. Christ knows it's time. These young arseholes have had it all their way for too long. Why should we always have to grit our teeth and take it like good sports? Why shouldn't we hand it out for a change? Artists of the world unite! We have nothing to lose but our Queensberry rules.' He punched the air.

'Don't be silly, Sam,' said Eleanor, like a mother to an over-excited child. Adrian picked up the *Sentinel Review* and sidled towards the door. 'Where are you going?' she demanded.

'To the loo, if I have your permission,' said Adrian.

Sam pointed to the newspaper in his hand. 'Are you taking that with you?'

'Something to read,' Adrian said as he went out of the room.

'Wipe your bottom on it!' Sam called after him.

'Sam, why get so upset?' said Eleanor. 'It's only a silly little article, by a silly little journalist.'

'But everybody I know will read it,' said Sam, pacing restlessly round the room. 'At this very moment sniggers are rising like sacrificial smoke from a thousand breakfast tables all across London and the Home Counties.' He picked up a pottery vase. 'This is nice. Did you make it?'

'Yes.'

'Very nice . . . Is it for sale?'

'Not to you, Sam. If you like it, have it as a present.'

'No way. Would a hundred be fair?'

'Far too much.'

'I'll give you seventy-five.' He took out his chequebook.

'That's very generous. I am selling the odd piece now, actually. It's very satisfying.'

'You have a real gift.' Sam sat down at the table to write the cheque. 'Ellie, tell me, am I really such a shit as that bitch makes out?'

Eleanor pretended that she had to think about this question. She looked at the ceiling and stroked her chin. 'Well . . .'

'All right, so I'm a bit vain,' said Sam, 'but I have every reason to be! Three BAFTAs, two Royal Television Society Awards, one Emmy, one Silver Nymph –'

'Silver Nymph?'

'From the Monte Carlo TV Festival, they give you a silver nymph. One Golden Turd from Luxemburg – at least, that's what it looked like. Here.' He gave her the cheque.

'Thank you, Sam.'

'And now that I'm writing real movies, maybe I'll win an Oscar!'

'What's your film about?' Eleanor asked.

'Florence Nightingale.'

'What do you know about Florence Nightingale?'

'More than the producers, which is the main thing.

Actually there is a script already. They want me to do a rewrite.'

'Will it have a scene with Florence Nightingale in the nude?' Eleanor inquired.

'You may mock, Ellie. But I shall get paid three hundred thousand dollars for a month's work. And have a house with pool in Beverly Hills to do it in.'

'Goodness!'

'But what use is my success, when I have nobody to share it with?' Sam cried, consciously hamming. 'I live all alone in my luxuriously furnished farmhouse, wading from room to room through the deep-pile carpet, listening to the ticking of the clocks, longing for the phone to ring.'

'You just said you were too busy to come and see us,' Eleanor pointed out.

'I'm busy *and* lonely. It's a well-known affliction in this day and age. And anyway . . .' Sam's speech tailed away into silence.

'What?'

'Well, it's hard to say it, Ellie, but, frankly, it embarrasses me to meet Adrian now. You remember what it was like in the old days. He was writing his novels, I was writing my plays. We used to swap stories about how our work was going. Now I come here and babble on about my projects and he has sod-all to say in return. It's like serving at tennis to an opponent with no arms.'

'Adrian doesn't mind.'

'Well, I mind. It makes me seem . . . boastful.'

'Surely not, Sam,' said Eleanor drily.

'He's stagnating. You're both stagnating.'

'No we're not,' said Eleanor. 'I have my ceramics. Adrian has his anthologies.'

'You never go anywhere.'

'Yes we do. We go for walks on the Downs. Or drive to the sea.'

'I don't mean walks and drives,' said Sam.

Eleanor began to recover the papers from under the sofa and to stack them tidily. 'If you mean first nights, launch parties, Groucho's, that sort of thing . . .' she said.

'Yes, I mean that sort of thing.'

'We've lost interest.'

'Adrian may have lost interest,' said Sam. 'You haven't. Otherwise, why do you take all these Sunday papers?'

Eleanor smiled wryly. '*Touché*.'

'If you were married to me, you would be *in* them, not just reading them.'

'This morning that doesn't seem such an inviting prospect,' said Eleanor.

'Oh. Yes,' said Sam. '*Touché.*' Being reminded of Fanny Tarrant's article plunged him into gloom. 'The bitch,' he said. Then, after a pause, 'Why has Adrian stopped writing?'

'He's only stopped writing novels. Sort of retired from it.'

'Writers don't retire. No one gives it up voluntarily.'

'He still writes nonfiction,' said Eleanor.

'You mean those anthologies? That's scissors and paste work.'

'They have introductions.'

'Yes, they have introductions,' said Sam. 'Ellie, for Christ's sake, Adrian Ludlow was the white hope of the English novel once!'

'Yes, well, that was a long time ago,' said Eleanor, as if firmly closing a drawer inadvertently opened. 'Sam, I don't like discussing Adrian with you like this, behind his back.'

Sam sidled up behind her and put his arm round her waist. 'If we were lovers it would seem more natural,' he said, half-jokingly.

Eleanor adroitly escaped from his embrace. 'Are you trying to get even with Laura?'

'Laura's history. It was a mistake from the beginning.'

'I always thought you were too old for her –'

'No, she was too young for me,' said Sam. 'But you're right. I need a mature woman.'

'You should have stuck with Georgina,' said Eleanor.

'Georgina should have stuck with me, you mean.' Sam frowned at this reminder of his first wife. 'I wonder if it was Georgina who told that bitch about my –' He stopped in mid-sentence.

'Toupée?' Eleanor said. Sam looked pained. 'Sorry, Sam, I shouldn't tease you. Not this morning.'

She gave him a conciliatory kiss on the cheek. He put his arms round her and kissed her on the lips. Eleanor half-responded, but after a moment or two pushed him away.

'No, Sam . . .'

'Why not?'

'You're just using me to salve your wounded ego.'

'No I'm not.'

'Yes you are. No other woman being available this early on a Sunday morning.'

'Ellie, not a day goes by but I don't wish you'd married me instead of Adrian.'

'Liar.'

'It's true!'

'Adrian asked me, you didn't.'

'But he cheated. We didn't believe in marriage in those days, remember?'

'I try not to.'

'We were going to start a commune.'

Eleanor gave a short, sarcastic laugh. 'Some commune it would have been, with two writers in it.'

'But Adrian saw that secretly you yearned for the old bourgeois certainties. I bet he even went down on his knees, didn't he?'

'Sam, I don't want to talk about those days,' Eleanor said vehemently. She seemed almost upset.

'All right,' said Sam, raising his hands placatingly.

'You should know why,' Eleanor said.

Adrian came in from the hall in time to hear this remark. He was dressed in tracksuit and trainers, with a towel round his neck, and held the *Sentinel* Review in one hand. 'Why what?' he said.

'Nothing,' said Eleanor. She busied herself putting the used breakfast things on a tray.

Sam looked Adrian up and down. 'Why are you wearing a tracksuit?'

'I usually go for a little jog on Sunday mornings and then have a sauna.'

'Don't tell me you still poach yourself in that foetid garden shed.'

'The facilities are much improved since you last

saw them,' said Adrian. 'It's a pity you haven't got time to join me.'

'No way. Saunas give me a rash.'

'What a shame,' said Adrian. 'It would do you good. Sweat Fanny Tarrant's poisons out of your system.'

'Adrian thinks the sauna is a universal panacea,' said Eleanor. 'Are you sure you wouldn't like some fresh coffee, Sam?'

'Some juice would be lovely, if you've got it.'

'Right.' Eleanor took the loaded tray into the kitchen.

Adrian put the *Sentinel* Review on the table. 'Well, I finished it,' he said.

'I don't blame you for being leery of her,' Sam said, 'but if you published your piece at the same time as hers, it would take the wind out of her sails.'

'I'm not afraid of Fanny Tarrant,' Adrian said.

'Or better still, *before* hers,' Sam said, ignoring Adrian's remark as he pursued his own train of thought. 'The *Sentinel* might not run her piece on you at all. And anyway –'

'Sam –'

'Anyway, the sales of your backlist will go up, whatever she says about you.'

'My sales are not bad, actually,' said Adrian. '*The Hideaway* is –'

'An "A" level set text. Yes, you said. But that's not going to make you rich, Adrian. Nor is another Paragon Book of Boring Crap. What you need is a telly serial and a tie-in paperback re-issue. Tell you what: I'll put *The Hideaway* up to the BBC for serialization.'

'They turned it down years ago,' Adrian said.

'Yes, but this time *I'd* be offering to do the script.'

'You could have offered before now.'

Sam looked a little uncomfortable. 'Well, I suppose I could've, but, you know how it is. I've been so *busy* . . .'

'Sam, you don't have to try and bribe me.'

'I'm not! I'm not,' Sam protested. 'Look, I'll pitch *The Hideaway* to the Beeb as soon as I get back from the States. I'll do it whether you go through with this Fanny Tarrant sting or not, honest. All I ask is that you think about it.' He looked at his watch. 'Christ, I must get going . . . Just think about it, OK?'

'I've already thought about it,' said Adrian. 'I'll do it.'

Sam stared. 'What?'

'I've been trying to tell you. I decided while I was in the loo. I'll do it.'

Eleanor, bearing a jug of orange juice and glasses on a tray, came through the kitchen door in time to hear this, and stopped in her tracks.

'Oh,' said Sam, wrongfooted by Adrian's announcement. 'Well, great!' he added. He glanced nervously at Eleanor, who was looking at Adrian.

'Do what?' she said. Adrian smiled blandly, but did not reply.

'I must dash, Ellie,' Sam said. 'Sorry about the juice.' He turned to Adrian. 'I'll phone Peter Reeves at the *Chronicle* and tell him to get in touch with you.'

'Right,' said Adrian.

'Let me know what happens. Are you on e-mail?'

'No,' said Adrian. 'But we have a fax. Same number as the telephone.'

'I'll fax you my contact numbers when I get to LA,' said Sam. 'I'll see myself out. *Ciao.*'

Sam waved to both, and scuttled from the room. Eleanor did not take her eyes off Adrian. 'Do what?' she repeated.

As Adrian opened his mouth to reply, Sam reappeared at the doorway leading to the hall.

'The thing is', he said to Adrian, 'to find her weak point, her Achilles' heel, her guilty secret.'

'Perhaps she hasn't got one,' Adrian said.

'Everybody's got one,' said Sam.

This remark appeared to have an effect greater than he had intended. Sam himself broke the charged

silence that followed. 'Well . . . 'bye,' he said. 'Ellie –
I'll collect the pot when I get back.'

'Sam, wait a minute!' said Eleanor.

'Sorry, must rush,' he said, and disappeared. They
heard the sound of the front door slamming behind
him.

Eleanor turned on Adrian. 'You don't mean to say
that you've agreed to that crazy idea? You're not going
to let Fanny Tarrant interview you?'

'If she really wants to,' Adrian said.

'Are you mad?'

'I don't think so.'

'You saw what she did to Sam. How will you feel
if she does it to you?'

'It won't bother me.'

'Oh, really? What makes you so confident?'

'Because I'm not competing any more. I'm outside
the game.'

'What game?'

'The fame game,' Adrian said. 'I've got nothing to
lose. Unlike Sam, I don't *care* what Fanny Tarrant says
about me.'

'So you think . . . Anyway, why should you fight
Sam's battles for him?'

'He says he'll adapt *The Hideaway* for the BBC,' said
Adrian.

'Nothing will come of it,' said Eleanor.

'I know,' said Adrian.

'So why are you doing this?'

'There'll be a fee, if it comes off . . . The *Chronicle* pays quite well, I believe. You could get that new kiln.'

Eleanor brushed aside this explanation. '*Why*, Adrian?'

He hesitated for a moment before replying. 'Well, you know I've been a bit stuck for a theme for my next anthology?'

'No, I didn't.'

'Well, I have. While I was in the loo just now, I had an idea: the *Paragon Book of Interviews*. From classical times to the present day. Starting with Socrates and Ion of Ephesus, and ending with Fanny Tarrant and the editor.'

Eleanor seemed only half-convinced. 'You'd include her interview with you?'

'It would be a rather novel twist, don't you think?'

'Supposing it's as nasty as her piece about Sam?'

'That would make it representative. And I would get the credit for being a jolly good sport.'

'Supposing she refused permission?'

'Then I might reprint my piece about her instead,' said Adrian. 'In any case, the experience of being interviewed by Fanny Tarrant would be very useful when I come to write my introduction.'

'I can't believe I'm hearing this,' Eleanor said. 'After all we've been through.' She looked around the room as if vainly seeking somebody to appeal to. 'And this "piece" of yours about her . . . what makes you think you can pull it off? You've never done anything like it before.'

'Yes I have. Those character sketches in the old *Mag* . . .'

'Adrian, that was student stuff!'

'It was good, though.'

Eleanor stared at him. 'I know what this is about,' she said.

'Ah, I sense a little psychoanalysis in the offing,' said Adrian. 'Let me adopt a suitable posture.' He stretched out on the *chaise longue*.

Eleanor was not deterred by his mockery. 'You're trying to get back to that golden time when you and Sam were best friends, not just old friends. When you both had the world before you.'

'Go on,' said Adrian, looking at the ceiling.

'When you were both on equal terms. Or perhaps you had the edge. Most people thought so. But now that Sam is so successful, and you're . . .' Eleanor searched for an appropriate word.

'A failure?' Adrian volunteered.

'I was going to say, semi-retired. Call it what you like, it's affected your relationship. You imagine that by doing this favour for Sam you'll get back on terms with him.'

'An ingenious theory,' Adrian said, getting to his feet. 'I must admit I feel a tingle of anticipation about this project that I haven't felt for a very long time. I never had much fun writing novels.'

'You needn't tell me,' said Eleanor.

Adrian glanced at his watch. 'I'd better go for my jog now, or there won't be time for a sauna before lunch.'

'You'll regret it.'

'No, I won't. I promise.'

He gave her a kiss on the cheek, and went out. Eleanor stared into space for a moment, with a troubled expression. Then she sat down at the table, unfolded the copy of the *Sentinel* Review and began to read Fanny Tarrant's article from the point at which she had been interrupted by Sam Sharp's visit.

2

On the Monday of the following week, in the late morning, Adrian awaited the arrival of Fanny Tarrant. He was alone in the cottage. The *Sentinel*'s photographer had come earlier, taken numerous pictures, and departed, leaving Adrian to replace the furniture he had disturbed. Everything had gone according to plan in the previous week. Adrian had told his agent, Geoffrey, of Fanny Tarrant's interest in interviewing him, and Geoffrey had spoken to Fanny and made the arrangements. Peter Reeves, features editor of the *Sunday Chronicle*, primed by Sam, had rung Adrian and expressed keen interest in a profile of the Invidious Interviewer. Adrian had received a fax from Sam giving his address and contact numbers in Los Angeles, and asking if there had been any developments, but Adrian had not replied. He told Eleanor that he was going to wait and see how the interview with Fanny Tarrant went before he committed himself to carrying out Sam's plot. Eleanor said she didn't want to hear about it. She arranged to spend the day of the interview with her niece, Rosemary, who lived in East Grinstead, and drove off just before the appointed hour, silent and disapproving. No sooner had the rasp of the Peugeot's corroded exhaust pipe faded, than Adrian heard the churning diesel engine of Fanny's approaching taxi. He ejected the Handel CD that had been playing softly on the hi-fi, and set the tape deck to record through a small free-standing microphone mounted on the bookshelves. The door-bell chimed just as he completed this task.

Adrian opened the door to a good-looking young woman in her late twenties or early thirties, with short blonde hair, expensively cut. She was smartly dressed, in a short skirt and tailored jacket, and carried a slimline black leather briefcase.

'Miss Tarrant?' he said.

'Yes.' She smiled faintly, as if amused by something, perhaps the formality of this mode of address.

'Please come in.'

He led her into the living room.

'Was that your wife who drove out of the gate as my taxi was trying to get in?' she said. Her accent might have been described as 'educated Estuary'.

'Yes. She's gone to visit her niece in East Grinstead.'

'Pity. I was hoping to meet her.'

'That was what she wanted to avoid,' said Adrian.

'Oh, why's that?' said Fanny.

'She reads your articles,' said Adrian. 'Won't you sit down?' Fanny chose the *chaise longue*. Adrian sat down in the armchair opposite. 'She particularly remembers the one about that art historian,' he said. 'Sir somebody double-barrelled.'

'Sir Robert Digby-Sisson?'

'That's the chap,' said Adrian. 'You commented adversely on Lady Digby-Sisson's fingernails.'

'Does your wife bite her fingernails?' Fanny said, in a tone of neutral inquiry.

'No,' said Adrian. 'She just didn't want to risk appearing in your article in some similarly disparaging aside.'

'It sounds as if she doesn't approve of your doing this interview,' said Fanny.

'No, she doesn't,' said Adrian.

Fanny opened her briefcase and took out a reporter's notebook and a small Sony cassette recorder. 'You don't mind if I use this?' she said, holding up the latter.

'Not at all. As long as you don't mind my using one too.'

'By all means,' said Fanny. She checked that her machine had a cassette tape in it, switched it on, and placed it on a coffee table positioned between them.

'D'you want to set up your tape recorder?' she said.

'It's already on.' He gestured at the hi-fi system.

'Oh, I see. It's rather a long way away.'

'It has a very sensitive microphone. Voice-activated. I hope yours is as good.'

'It's state of the art,' she said. 'Why do you want to record the interview?'

'To settle any disputes that might arise about what I said.'

'Fair enough,' said Fanny. She opened her notebook and took a ballpen out of her briefcase. She looked round the room. 'This is nice. Have you been here long.'

'It used to be our weekend retreat,' said Adrian, 'but it was smaller then. When we decided to leave London, we bought the adjoining cottage and knocked through the party wall.'

Fanny made some notes, evidently about the furnishings and decor of the room. 'Do you collect ceramics?' she said. 'There seem to be a lot of them.'

'My wife made them,' said Adrian. 'She took up pottery when we moved here.'

'You've been married quite a long time, haven't you?' she said, as she wrote.

'I suppose so. By modern standards.'

'And you've got two sons?'

'They're grown up now – flown the nest. Are you married yourself?'

'No,' Fanny said.

'But you must have a . . . what's the approved term nowadays?'

'Partner.'

'Ah, yes,' said Adrian. 'What's his name?'

'Creighton,' said Fanny.

'Spelled . . .?' Adrian asked.

'C, r, e, i, g, h, t, o, n.' Fanny looked up from her notebook. 'Why do you ask?'

'And what does Mr Creighton do?'

'Creighton is his first name,' she said.

'Really? You mean, he was christened "Creighton"?'

'I'm not sure he was ever christened,' she said.

'Oh. A heathen, eh?'

'There are quite a lot of them about, you know,' said Fanny. 'Would you describe yourself as a Christian?'

'Well, I attend the parish church at Christmas, harvest festival, that sort of thing,' said Adrian. 'I contribute to the roofing fund. I believe in the Church of England as an institution. I'm not sure about the doctrine. I don't think the vicar is, either, as a matter of fact . . . And yourself?' he added.

'I was brought up as a Catholic,' she said, 'but I haven't been to church for years.'

'How did you lose your faith?'

Fanny sighed. 'Look, this is going to take a very long time if you keep asking *me* questions.'

Adrian smiled sweetly. 'I've got all day.'

'All right,' said Fanny. 'So have I. But what about Mrs Ludlow?'

'She won't be back till this evening.'

'I see,' said Fanny. 'By the way, did everything go all right with Freddy?' Adrian looked blank. 'The photographer.'

'Oh yes. Fine, I think . . . Funny business though, isn't it, photography.'

'What's funny about it?' Fanny said.

'Well, they come into your house, move all your furniture about . . .' Adrian, noticing that a picture on the wall was askew, got up and went across the room to straighten it. 'They set up their lights and tripods and umbrellas and circus hoops all over the place –'

Fanny frowned. 'Circus hoops?'

'Those folding things for reflecting light . . . Then they make you twist yourself into the most artificial postures and talk to you all the time like a barber, and keep telling you not to look so serious –'

'Did Freddy tell you not to look serious?'

'No, but they usually do,' said Adrian. 'I mean, they usually did in the days when I was photographed for book jackets.' He returned to his armchair.

'Freddy doesn't meddle with his subjects' natural expressions,' said Fanny. 'That's why he's a first-class portrait photographer.'

'Pretty extravagant with film, though, isn't he?'

'I think the paper can afford it,' said Fanny drily.

'No doubt. But why take so many pictures of the same face?'

'To find the one that tells you most about the subject. People's expressions are always changing, but so subtly and so fast that you don't know what you've captured until you develop the film.' She spoke with decision, as if she had thought about this question before. 'That's why photographs are more revealing than real life,' she said.

'And interviews,' Adrian said, 'are they more revealing than real life?'

'Interviews *are* real life. Mine are, anyway.'

'Oh, come!' Adrian protested.

'I invent nothing. That's why I use a tape recorder.'

'But you won't report *everything* I say, will you? You'll leave out the less interesting bits.'

'Obviously,' said Fanny. 'Otherwise it would be far too long, and very boring to read.'

'But you falsify a conversation if you leave out any part of it,' said Adrian. 'The dull bits, the hesitant bits, the repetitions, the silences.'

'There haven't been any silences yet.'

'There will be,' said Adrian. He locked on to her gaze and held it without blinking.

'All right,' said Fanny, after half a minute had passed in silence. 'I concede the point. An interview is not an exact record of reality. It's a selection. An interpretation.'

'It's a game,' said Adrian

'A game?'

'A game for two players,' said Adrian. 'The question is, what are the rules, and how does one win? Or lose, as the case may be.' He smiled genially. 'Coffee? There's some on the hob in the kitchen already made.'

'Thank you,' said Fanny.

'How do you take it?'

'Black. No sugar.'

'Very wise,' said Adrian, as he went into the kitchen. Fanny sat still until he returned, bearing two cups of coffee on a tray.

'Actually,' said Fanny, as if their conversation had not been interrupted, 'I don't see it as a game. I see it as a transaction. A barter. The interviewer gets copy. The interviewee gets publicity.'

'But I don't want publicity,' said Adrian.

'Why did you agree to be interviewed, then?'

'Why did you want to interview me?' he asked.

'I asked first,' said Fanny.

'All right. I was curious.'

'Curious about what?'

'About why you want to interview me.' Fanny acknowledged the parry with a wry smile. 'You usually interview celebrities,' Adrian said. 'I haven't been a celebrity for years, if I ever was one. So why me?'

'I'm curious too,' said Fanny, ' about why you aren't a celebrity any more. Why you stopped writing, why you dropped out of the literary world.'

'I still publish books,' he said.

'Yes, I know. The Paragon anthologies. Anybody could do them.'

'Well, not quite anybody,' he said with mild pique. 'You have to be able to *read*. You have to know where to look for things.'

'You see, your fiction meant a great deal to me once,' she said.

'Really?'

'I read *The Hideaway* when I was fifteen,' she said. 'It was the first time a modern novel really excited me. I still think it's the best treatment of adolescence in postwar British fiction.'

'Well, thank you. Thank you very much.' Adrian could not disguise his pleasure at this compliment. 'It's an "A" level set text, you know,' he said.

'God, what a depressing thought,' said Fanny.

'Oh, why?'

'Well, the whole point of *The Hideaway* for me was that it wasn't a set text, it wasn't prep, it wasn't examination fodder. It was something private, secret, subversive.'

'I know what you mean,' he said, smiling.

'Can't you stop them teaching it?'

'I don't think I can,' said Adrian. 'Anyway, the royalties come in useful.'

'There was a group of us at school,' Fanny reminisced. 'We were like a secret society. We used to read *The Hideaway* aloud and argue about it – not in a lit-crit way, but about who we liked best – Maggie or Steve or Alex – and about what would've happened to them after the story ended. It was like a religion. *The Hideaway* was our bible.'

Adrian stared. 'Good Lord. How long did that last?'

'A whole term. A summer term.'

'Then in the holidays you read another book and based a new religion on that?'

'No, there was never another book like *The Hide-*

away,' she said. 'I've brought my much-thumbed copy for you to sign, actually, if you wouldn't mind.'

'Of course.'

Fanny took an old Penguin edition of *The Hideaway*, with a soiled cover and yellowing pages, from her briefcase and handed it to Adrian. He wrote on the flyleaf: *To Fanny Tarrant, with best wishes, Adrian Ludlow.*

'You were at a boarding school, then?' he said as he wrote.

'How did you guess?'

'You said "prep" rather than "homework".' He handed the book back to Fanny, who glanced at the inscription.

'Thanks,' she said, and put the book back in her briefcase.

'I thought you went to a comprehensive school in Basildon,' he said.

'Who told you that?' she said.

'Sam Sharp.'

'I was wondering when his name would crop up,' said Fanny. 'The trouble with Mr Sharp is that he doesn't listen to what anybody says to him. What I actually said was, that I *wished* I'd gone to a comprehensive school in Basildon.'

'Why?'

'It would have been a better preparation for journalism than a convent boarding school in Hampshire,' she said. 'Could we get back to you? Why did you stop writing fiction?'

'I decided that my *oeuvre* was complete. That I had nothing more to say.'

'Just like that?' she said.

'Just like that,' he said.

'Didn't it worry you?'

'For a while. Then I began to enjoy it.'

'How?'

'It's like when you run out of petrol and your car stops,' Adrian said. 'At first it's annoying, but after a while you come to appreciate the silence and tranquillity. You hear things you never heard before because they were drowned by the noise of the engine. You see things that previously flashed by in a blur.'

'Have you ever actually run out of petrol?' Fanny said.

'Since you ask, no.'

'I thought so,' she said.

'It was a figure of speech.'

'Doesn't it bother you, when you see your contemporaries still writing and publishing?'

'On the contrary. There are far too many writers around who have nothing more to say, but insist on saying it again and again, in book after book, year after year.'

'Which writers are you thinking of?' she said.

'The same ones that you're thinking of,' he said.

Her expression was amused, but sceptical. 'I can't believe you gave it up so easily,' she said.

Adrian took a deep breath. 'You mean, how could I give up all those long, solitary hours spent staring at a blank page, or out of the window, gnawing the end of a ballpoint, trying to create something out of nothing, to will creatures with no previous existence into being, to give them names, parents, education, clothes, possessions . . . having to decide whether they have blue eyes or brown, straight hair or curly hair or no hair – God, the tedium of it! And then the grinding, ball-breaking effort of forcing it all into words – fresh-seeming words, words that don't sound as if you bought them second-hand as a job lot . . . And then having to set the characters moving, behaving, inter-acting with each other in ways that will seem simul-taneously interesting, plausible, surprising, funny and moving.' He ticked off these epithets on his fingers. 'It's like playing chess in three dimensions,' he said. 'It's absolute hell. Would *you* miss it?'

'I'd miss the end result,' she said, 'the satisfaction

of having created something permanent. The effect you have on other people.'

'But you don't know, most of the time, what the effect is. Writing novels is like putting messages into bottle after bottle and tossing them into the sea on the outgoing tide without any idea of where they'll be washed up or how they will be interpreted.' He added, 'I *have* done that with bottles, by the way.'

'What about reviews?' said Fanny.

'What indeed,' said Adrian, after a moment's hesitation.

'Don't they give you some feedback?'

'They tell you a lot about the reviewer. Not much about your book,' he said.

'My first job in journalism was writing film reviews, for a listings magazine,' she said. 'I don't think I gave away much about myself.'

'They weren't as cruel as your interviews, then?' he said.

Fanny laughed dismissively. 'Cruel?'

'Sir Robert Digby-Sisson thought you were cruel. According to a rival journal, he wept on reading your interview with him.'

'He wept while he was *giving* the interview,' she said. 'He's a big cry-baby. Tears gush from his eyes at the slightest pretext. When he wasn't blubbing into his handkerchief, he was trying to grope me.'

'You didn't mention that in your article,' said Adrian.

'I did, but it was cut. The lawyers were nervous because I didn't have a witness. This thing', she pointed to her tape recorder, 'doesn't pick up the sound of a knee being squeezed.'

'You were cruel to my friend Sam Sharp, too,' said Adrian. 'He was very hurt.'

'He'll survive,' said Fanny.

'Yes, I dare say he will,' said Adrian.

'Though I admit I *was* a little surprised when you agreed to see me just after that piece appeared,' she said. 'I thought it might be a trap.'

Adrian could not suppress a start. 'A trap? What kind of trap?'

'I thought perhaps Mr Sharp might be lurking in the house somewhere.'

Adrian laughed heartily. 'Oh no, Sam's in Los Angeles. But what did you think he would do? Assault you?'

'It has been known,' said Fanny. 'You know Brett Daniel?'

'The actor?'

'The week after I published my interview with him

he deliberately spilled a glass of red wine down the front of my dress at a first-night party. Then he followed it with a white-wine chaser on the grounds that it would take the stain out.'

'Well, that does work, actually . . .' said Adrian. 'Did you sue him?'

'I sent him a whopping bill for a new dress. But he told all his cronies it was worth every penny.'

'You didn't think that Sam was going to leap out at you here, flinging glasses of wine, did you?' said Adrian.

'I thought he might leap out flinging insults,' said Fanny.

Adrian steepled his hands and pressed the fingertips against his chin. 'Doesn't it bother you, knowing that most of the people you've interviewed hate you afterwards?' he said.

'It's part of the job,' she said, with a shrug.

'It's a funny sort of job, though, isn't it? Character assassination.'

'Are you trying to wind me up?' she said.

'No, no! But you must admit, your pieces are usually pretty destructive. Isn't that what your readers expect of you?'

'They expect good journalism,' said Fanny, 'and I hope I give it to them. What do you think about the younger generation of British novelists?'

'I try not to think of them,' said Adrian. 'But you're not telling me, are you, that all those readers would be turning eagerly to your page if you were billed as, *Fanny Tarrant – Britain's Kindest Interviewer*?'

'No, I'm not telling you that,' said Fanny. 'I'm trying, with some difficulty, to interview you.'

'Your readers wouldn't stoop to reading about the bonking escapades of footballers and pop stars in the tabloids. But you give them the same kind of pleasure in a more refined form, by making the great and the good look silly.'

'They do it unassisted,' she said. 'I just report it.'

'Tell me,' said Adrian, in the tone of one sincerely seeking enlightenment, 'when you've written one of your really nasty pieces, like the one on Sam –'

'Oh, I can be much nastier than that,' Fanny interjected.

'I don't doubt it,' said Adrian with a smile. 'But when you've written a piece like that, and it's printed, do you imagine the victim reading it? I mean, do you imagine poor old Sam, say, getting up on Sunday morning, and padding down the hall in his dressing gown and slippers, and picking up the *Sunday Sentinel* off the doormat, and taking it into the kitchen to read with his first cup of tea, and riffling through the pages of the Review section to find your interview, and smiling as he sees Freddy's full-page colour photo of him sitting at his Apple Mac, and then starting to read the text, and the sudden fading of his smile as he comes to the first sneer, and then the thumping of his heart, the spasm in the gut, the rush of adrenalin to the bloodstream, as it dawns on him that the piece is *all* sneers, that he has been well and truly stitched up. I mean, do you imagine all that? Does it give you a kick? Is that why you do this job?'

Fanny for the first time that morning looked slightly rattled. 'Could we get back to me asking the questions?' she said coldly.

'Why?'

'It's customary. The interviewer asks the questions and the interviewee answers them.'

'But that's why the interview is such an artificial form,' he said. 'It isn't a real dialogue. It's an interrogation.'

'Well, interrogation has its uses,' she said.

'Such as what?'

'Such as uncovering the truth.'

'Oh, the truth . . .' said Adrian. '"*What is truth?*" said *jesting Pilate, and would not stay for an answer.* Did it never occur to you that my questions might reveal more than my answers?'

'I prefer to stick to my own agenda, thanks.'

'So you won't quote the question I just asked you?'

'I've no idea what I'm going to quote yet,' Fanny said irritably.

'I suppose you have to listen to the whole tape first,' said Adrian.

'I have a transcript made.'

'And then you edit it on a word processor?' he said. 'Or do you write the first draft in longhand?'

'You *are* winding me up, aren't you?' she said.

'No! No.' Adrian protested.

'That's straight out of the handbook for intellectually challenged journalists,' said Fanny. '*One Hundred Boring Questions to Ask an Author.* "Do you write something every day? Do you write with a fountain pen or on a computer? Do you work out the whole story before you start?"'

Adrian gave a smile of recognition, and said, '"Are your novels autobiographical?"'

'No, that's not a boring question,' Fanny said.

'Well, I always used to give a boring answer,' he said. '"*My novels are a mixture of personal experience, observation of other people, and imagination. I like to think that my readers won't be able to tell which is which, and sometimes I'm not too sure myself.*"'

'That's not a boring answer either, actually,' said Fanny, making a note.

'Why do you make notes if you've got a tape recorder?' he asked. 'Belt and braces? In case your battery gives out?'

'The machine records your words,' she said, 'the notebook my comments.'

'Ah,' he said. 'Can I have a look?' He stretched out his hand.

'No,' she said. 'What's your earliest memory?'

'My earliest memory . . . hmm . . .' He thought for a moment. 'Well, it was a false memory really. Of looking up at the sky at flying fortresses.'

'You mean bombers?' said Fanny.

'Yes. American B17s. It was the very end of the war. I was sitting in my pushchair. My mother had taken me for an airing to the local park – we were living in Kent, Faversham, at the time, and planes were often flying overhead, but this must have been a particularly big raid, a thousand-bomber job, all flying in formation. It was a bright, clear day. Suddenly the air was filled with a powerful throbbing, growling noise, as if the whole sky was vibrating with the sound of a single, gigantic engine. All the people in the park stopped what they were doing and looked up, shading their eyes. I started to cry. I was frightened by the noise, I suppose. My mother said. "It's all right Adrian, it's only the Flying Fortresses." I squinted up at the sky. The planes were too high to be visible, all you could see was their white vapour trails, ruled like chalk lines across the blue sky. But I somehow convinced myself that I could see them. Only what I thought I saw were not airplanes, but fortresses – square, solid buildings, with drawbridges and battlements and flags fluttering, sailing magically across the sky. I nurtured this idea for some years, until I went to infant school, and drew a picture of my flying fortresses, and the teacher laughed at me when I explained what they were.'

'That's a very nice story,' said Fanny.

'Thank you,' said Adrian.

'Only you weren't born until two years after the war,' she said.

'Quite right,' said Adrian.

'And that memory belongs to the hero of your second novel.'

'Right again,' said Adrian. 'I was just testing you.'

'Since I've passed the test, perhaps we could stop playing games and get on with the interview?'

'What about a spot of lunch first?' he said.

'Lunch?' Fanny did not sound enthusiastic.

'Yes. Ellie left us some cold cuts and salad in the fridge. And I could open a tin of soup.'

'I don't usually eat lunch,' she said, 'but if you're hungry, I'll sit down with you and nibble something while we go on talking.'

'You don't eat lunch?' said Adrian. 'But Sam was particularly outraged that you attacked him after eating the delicious poached salmon he prepared for you.'

'He ate most of it himself, actually,' said Fanny. 'And drank most of the wine. But please – if you want to eat – go ahead.'

'No, it doesn't matter,' said Adrian. 'I often skip lunch myself, as a matter of fact. I'm on a diet. I've become more health-conscious since I gave up writing novels.'

'That's interesting,' said Fanny. 'Why is that, d'you think?'

'I suppose while I was pursuing literary immortality I didn't think much about mortality,' said Adrian. 'When I was a novelist I had a pipe in my mouth all day, ate fried breakfasts, drank the greater part of a bottle of wine over dinner and hardly ever took any exercise. Now I scrutinize every packet of food for E numbers, eschew salt and sugar, measure my alcohol intake in units, and jog every day. My only indulgence is the sauna.'

'I wouldn't describe a sauna as an indulgence,' said Fanny.

'But the feeling afterwards – don't you find it euphoric?' said Adrian.

'The only time I tried it, I hated it,' she said.

'Where was that?' Adrian asked.

'Oh . . . some hotel "leisure complex",' she said.

'I expect you wore a swimming costume.'

'Yes, of course.'

'But you mustn't wear anything in the sauna!' he said vehemently. 'It constricts the body, interferes with the sweating. It's totally wrong.'

'I didn't have any choice,' she said. 'It was a mixed sauna, right next to the swimming pool.'

'I know,' said Adrian, shaking his head. 'I bet it was full of people who squelched in straight from the pool and sat there giving out clouds of chlorinated steam . . .'

Fanny did not deny it.

'The English really have no idea how to take a sauna,' said Adrian. 'It's enough to make you weep.'

'How should you do it, then?' Fanny asked.

Adrian leaned forward in his chair and spoke with the intensity of a devotee. 'First you take a warm shower. Then you dry off. Then you bathe your feet and ankles in a warm footbath, to help the circulation. Then you enter the sauna, and sit or lie on a bench – the higher it is the hotter it is – for ten or fifteen minutes, until the sweat is breaking out all over your body in beads. Then you take a long cold shower, or plunge into an icy lake if there's one handy, walk about a bit in the fresh air, and then wrap yourself up in a bathrobe and relax somewhere warm.' He sighed. 'There's nothing like it.'

Fanny was obviously intrigued. 'Where do you go to do this?' she said.

'Into my back garden,' he said.

'You mean, you have your own sauna here?'

'Oh yes,' he said. 'There's no lake, alas, but I've just built an annexe with a shower and a cold plunge bath. Would you like to see it?' He gestured towards the back of the house.

'Later perhaps,' said Fanny.

Adrian stared at her with the gleam of an idea in his eyes. 'In fact . . . you could try it out. If I can't offer you lunch, we could have a sauna instead.'

It was Fanny's turn to stare. 'I beg your pardon?' she said.

'You could discover what a real sauna is like,' he said.

'No thank you.'

'Why not?'

'I don't usually interview people in the nude,' she said.

'Oh, one doesn't *talk* in the sauna,' said Adrian. 'One communes silently with the heat. Afterwards one may talk.'

Fanny was silent. She looked at him as if trying to read his thoughts.

'What are you afraid of?' Adrian said. 'I would hardly risk being exposed in the *Sunday Sentinel* as a sex maniac, would I?'

'You know, I could make a good deal just out of this proposition,' she said

'Yes, you could,' he said. '"*Adrian Ludlow invited me to try his private sauna as casually as one might offer a visitor a drink. He assured me I wouldn't need a swimming costume. I made my excuses and left.*"'

'I have no intention of leaving,' Fanny said. 'I haven't finished my interview. I have a lot more questions to get through.'

'Forget them,' Adrian said.

'What?'

'Tear them up. Let's start again, after a sauna. Not an interview. No set questions, and set answers. No disguises. No pretences. No games. Just a conversation that takes its own course. What do you say?'

Fanny looked hard at Adrian. He did not flinch.

'I'll get you a bathrobe and towel and show you where to change,' he said, getting up.

'What makes you think I've agreed?' she said.

'Haven't you?' he said.

Fanny got slowly to her feet. 'I shall wrap the towel round me,' she said.

'Please yourself,' he said.

Fanny lingered, picking up and switching off the tape recorder and replacing it on the coffee table. Adrian held open the kitchen door. 'It's through here,' he said.

Fanny seemed to come to a decision. She straightened up, crossed the room and went through the door, without looking at Adrian. He followed her, and closed the door behind them.

3

Some forty minutes later, Fanny was back in the living room of the cottage, reclining on the *chaise longue*, wrapped in a white towelling bathrobe. Her hair was damp, her feet bare, her eyes closed. A plane droned overhead. Adrian came in through the kitchen door, also wearing a white towelling bathrobe and with rubber flip-flops on his feet, carrying a tray with a carton of orange juice and two tumblers on it. He looked across at Fanny as he put the tray down on the table.

'How do you feel?' he said.

'Blissful,' said Fanny, opening her eyes. 'You've made a convert.'

'Good.' Adrian poured two glasses of orange juice.

'You were quite right,' said Fanny. 'It *is* much more comfortable when you're naked.'

Adrian smiled complacently. 'You should have a drink now, to replace the fluid you lost,' he said. He handed her a glass of juice.

'Thanks,' she said, sitting up on the *chaise longue* to drink. 'How were you initiated yourself?'

'At a Writers' Conference in the middle of Finland years ago. We were offered a choice of excursions: a guided tour of the town, which looked about as exciting as Milton Keynes, or a traditional smoke sauna at a nearby lake. I chose the smoke sauna.'

'What's that?' Fanny stretched out a hand to switch on her tape recorder.

Adrian leaned down towards the little machine and announced with mock formality: 'A Smoke Sauna.' He continued in a normal voice. 'They heat up the cabin with a wood fire and let it fill with smoke. Then they open a trap-door in the roof just long enough to let the smoke escape, but not the heat. When you go in, the whole place smells deliciously of charred wood. The walls and benches are covered with soot, and soon you are too. The heat is tremendous. Sweat pours down your body in rivulets.'

'Making streaks in the soot.'

'Exactly. There were all these famous writers crammed into the cabin, haunch to haunch, looking like savages in warpaint and smelling like barbecued spare ribs.'

'Men and women together?'

'No, the Finns were surprisingly prudish about that.

Not what you expect from Scandinavians. The ladies had a separate session and we joined them for beer and sausages later.'

'It sounds like fun.'

'Yes, it was. And on another day there was a football match between Finnish writers and the Rest of the World, played by the light of the midnight sun.'

'Who won?'

'We did, 3–2. Graham Swift turned out to be quite a good sweeper, I recall.'

'Do you still go to these literary junkets?' Fanny asked.

'I don't get invited any more,' he said.

'Being stuck in a country cottage under the Gatwick flight paths must seem rather a dull life in comparison.'

'Not at all,' said Adrian. 'It's a source of deep satisfaction to me to reflect that I need never be part of those anxious heaving masses in airport terminals again. Especially at this time of the year.'

'I know, I dread it. But I need my holiday.'

'What kind of holiday?'

'A very conventional kind. I like to lie in the sun beside a pool all day with a pile of paperbacks to hand and frequent long, cool drinks. We're going to Turkey this year. What about you?'

'We don't take holidays as such any more,' said Adrian.

'No holidays!'

'It's surprising what you can do without, you know, when you give it a try. Foreign holidays. New cars. New clothes. Second houses. Getting and spending. It's no way to live, really.'

'You gave all that up when you gave up writing novels?'

'That's right. It's called "downshifting". I read an article about it.'

'Downshifting is quite a recent phenomenon,' said Fanny.

'We were pioneers.'

'And it started in America.'

'No, it started here,' Adrian said firmly. 'Where do you live?'

'In a loft apartment in Clerkenwell.'

'Which you share with Creighton?'

'Yes.'

'What does he do?'

'He's a solicitor.'

'Oh. So Creighton would be useful if one of your victims decided to sue you.'

'He's a commercial lawyer,' said Fanny. 'And I wish you wouldn't keep using that word.'

'Creighton?' Adrian said.

'Victims. People in public life must expect to get a few knocks. And other people enjoy seeing them get roughed up a bit.'

'Ah! You admit that, then?'

'Of course, it's human nature. When you read my piece about Sam Sharp, didn't you feel – as well as sympathy and outrage and all the other things a friend should feel – didn't you feel an undercurrent of delicious pleasure too? The truth, now. "No disguises, no pretences."'

She leaned forward intently and compelled him to look her in the eye.

'All right! All right!' said Adrian. 'I admit it.'

Fanny relaxed with a sigh of satisfaction. 'Thank you.'

'But what a terrible admission to make,' said Adrian. 'How I hate you for making me enjoy my friend's suffering.'

'"Suffering" is rating Sam Sharp's bruised ego a bit high, isn't it?' Fanny said.

'You're very cynical for one so young,' said Adrian. 'Don't you ever feel even the faintest spasm of remorse when you see your articles in print?'

'No.'

'Truthfully, now.' He copied her inquisitorial manner.

'Why should I?' she said. 'I perform a valuable cultural function.'

'Oh. What is that?'

'There's such a lot of hype nowadays, people confuse success with real achievement. I remind them of the difference.'

'Does that entail making fun of their toupées and cowboy boots?'

'Sometimes it's the only way to penetrate their egotism. Your friend Mr Sharp has a certain talent, but he doesn't work hard enough to perfect it. He writes too much, too fast. Why?'

'He has an ex-wife to support. Two ex-wives.'

'The more he earns, the more alimony he has to pay. It's not the need for money that makes him over-produce, it's laziness.'

'Sam – *lazy*?'

'Yes. By keeping the scripts spilling out of his computer, like cars rolling off a production line, he never gives himself time to assess the quality of what he's producing. If he gets a bad review he can shrug it off because he's already working on the next project. The people he works for are not going to give him objective criticism. They're only interested in costs and deadlines and viewing figures. That's where I come in – to question the nature of his "success". His next screenplay will be a little better than it otherwise might have been, because of the pinpricks I inflicted on his ego the other day.'

'Hmm,' said Adrian.

'You sound sceptical,' said Fanny.

'Well, Sam and I go back a long way. It would take more than pinpricks to change him.'

'You were at university together, weren't you?' said Fanny.

'Yes. We were put in the same tutorial group in our first week. We became inseparable. Shared a flat together, edited a magazine together, wrote revue sketches together, got drunk together . . .'

'There's a scene at the end of one of your novels, where two undergraduates get drunk after their Finals . . .'

'*Salad Years.*' Adrian laughed at the memory. 'Yes, that was us. I came out of the Union, and there was Sam, weaving about in the middle of the campus, a bottle in his hand, looking for me. We'd been drinking all afternoon, but had got separated somehow. When he saw me, his face lit up in delight, and he waved and tried to run towards me. Only he was so drunk that his brain completely screwed up the message it was trying to send to his legs. Instead of carrying him towards me, they went into reverse, and he started running backwards. I could see his face filling with bewilderment and alarm, as if he was being abducted by some invisible force, but the harder he strained to run towards me, the faster he ran backwards, until eventually he overbalanced and fell flat on his back in a flowerbed. It was the funniest thing I ever saw in my life.' Adrian laughed again. 'At least, it seemed so at the time,' he said, conscious that Fanny was not laughing quite as much.

'Yes, it *is* funny in the book,' she said. 'But sad, too. The hero feels it's a . . . kind of . . .'

'Portent.'

'Yes. Of how they're going to grow distant from each other in the years to come.'

'That's the benefit of hindsight,' said Adrian. 'I didn't feel it at the time.'

'But was that what happened? With you and Sam Sharp?'

'It's inevitable. That sort of friendship belongs to youth. It can't survive into adult life. Your lives begin to diverge: you start separate careers, get married, raise families . . .'

'Would you say there was a homosexual element in your friendship at college?' said Fanny.

'Good God, no!' said Adrian emphatically.

'I don't mean anything overtly physical,' she said, 'but some unconscious homoerotic attraction?'

'Absolutely not,' said Adrian.

'Why does the suggestion bother you so much?' said Fanny.

'Ah, I spy the Freudian double-bind,' said Adrian. 'Yes means yes, and no means I'm in denial. You're barking up the wrong tree, I'm afraid. We were both in love with Ellie, most of the time.'

'Ellie?'

'My wife,' said Adrian curtly. He looked as if he already regretted having introduced her name.

'Oh, I see,' said Fanny. 'Oh, I *see*! So your wife is the girl in *Salad Years* – what's her name, Fiona?'

'No, no, Eleanor is a quite different sort of person,' Adrian said.

'But she occupied the same position vis-à-vis you and Sam, as Fiona does with the two young men in the novel?'

'Up to a point,' said Adrian.

'In the book, they actually *share* Fiona for a time,' Fanny said. 'She sleeps with both of them.'

'Look, I'd rather not discuss this any more, if you don't mind,' said Adrian.

'I thought this conversation was to take its own course,' Fanny said.

'As far as I'm concerned, yes. This concerns Ellie.'

'So she did sleep with both of you?'

'I didn't say that.'

'You wouldn't be so defensive about it if she hadn't.'

Adrian was silent, as he considered whether to say any more. 'No, I'm sorry,' he said at length, shaking his head.

'Off the record,' Fanny said. She reached out and switched off her tape recorder.

'What use is it to you off the record?'

'I told you, my interest is more than just pro-fessional.'

'How do I know I can trust you?'

'I trusted you when I went into the sauna,' said Fanny. 'How did *I* know?'

Adrian hesitated for a few moments. Then he said, 'All right, I'll tell you. But it's absolutely off the record.'

'Absolutely.' Fanny drew up her knees under her bathrobe, like a child about to be told a story.

'Sam and I wrote a revue for the Drama Society in our second year, and Ellie turned up for an audition. We fell for her at once, and she took to us. Both of us. Sam and I didn't want to fall out over her, so we got in the habit of going around together as a threesome. People in our peer group couldn't quite work out what was going on between us. We enjoyed keeping them guessing.'

'And what *was* going on?' Fanny asked.

'Nothing, sexually. We used to sit around smoking pot, and sometimes there would be a cuddling session *à trois*, but nothing more. Then one day Sam got a message that his father was seriously ill and had to dash home. Ellie and I were alone together for the first time. One night we got very mellow on some good weed and ended up in my bed. When Sam came back – his father recovered – we felt we had to tell him. He was furious. He accused us both of betraying him, of destroying the wonderful, unique relationship we'd had between the three of us. Ellie and I tried to tell Sam that we hadn't planned it, that it had just happened, but he wouldn't be mollified. Until . . .' Adrian paused.

'Until Ellie offered to sleep with him too,' said Fanny.

'Yes. She said that then we'd all be back on equal terms. I'll never forget Sam's face when she said it . . . We were both lost in wonderment, as a matter of fact. It seemed such a magnanimous gesture. It seemed to abolish the jealousy thing, the possessiveness thing, at a stroke. It was the sixties, you know: we thought we were reinventing sexual relationships. So the next night I made myself scarce, and Ellie went to bed with Sam. He and I never discussed it afterwards, and we went back to being a chaste, platonic threesome. But of course it wasn't the same. We had eaten the apple, or at least taken a large bite out of it. Eventually, Ellie had to choose between us.'

'In the novel', said Fanny, 'the girl goes on sleeping with both of the men for quite a long time.'

'That's all invented. There usually is more sex in fiction than in life, haven't you noticed?' said Adrian. 'Anyway, after a great deal of frustration, unhappy experiments with other relationships, and so on, Ellie chose me. In the novel, of course, she doesn't marry either of them, and they all go their different ways.'

Fanny waited to see if Adrian had anything more to add, but he didn't. 'That was fascinating,' she said. 'Thank you.'

'Now I think you should tell me something equally . . . personal, about yourself,' he said.

'Why?'

'It seems only fair.'

'All right,' she said. 'What d'you want to know?'

'Well . . . tell me about your tattoo.'

Fanny looked a little self-conscious. 'My butterfly?'

'I couldn't help noticing it just now . . .' He gestured in the direction of the sauna. 'Did you have it done for the Essex girl inside you struggling to get out?'

'No, I did it to please my boyfriend,' said Fanny.

'Creighton?'

'God, no, it was years ago,' she said. 'I was between school and university. I went a bit wild, that year. His name was Bruce. He was a rock musician, covered in tattoos. He kept on at me to have one too, and I was so besotted that I agreed. It's a real bore. Means I can't wear sleeveless dresses in the summer.'

'Oh, I think it's rather charming. It looks as if the butterfly has just alighted on your shoulder.'

'Unfortunately it's got Bruce's initials stencilled on its wings.'

'I didn't notice that.'

'It tends to become a tedious conversational topic at cocktail parties, if visible.'

'Yes, I can see that could be embarrassing. Is it quite irremovable?'

'Short of a skin graft, yes.' She pulled her bathrobe off one shoulder to squint at the tattoo. 'It hasn't faded a bit. Bruce branded me for life, damn him.'

Adrian stood close to Fanny to examine the tattoo. 'B. B.,' he said.

'Bruce Baxter.'

'Did it hurt?'

'It was agony.'

'And now?'

'Oh, I feel nothing now,' she said.

'It's rather exquisitely done, you know.' Adrian traced the outline of the tattoo with his finger.

It was the first time he had touched her, apart from the formal handshake at the front door, and it was an intimate touch, on the threshold of the erotic. Both showed they were aware of the liminal nature of the moment by their sudden stillness, so still that they might have been figures sculpted on a classical frieze. Adrian left his fingertip lightly pressing Fanny's skin, as he studied the butterfly like a curious lepidopterist. Fanny focused her gaze on his fingertip. Neither spoke. It was Eleanor who spoke.

'Am I interrupting something?' she said, from the kitchen door.

Adrian whirled round, and leaped away from the *chaise longue*. Fanny pulled the bathrobe back over her shoulder and stood up.

'Ellie!' Adrian exclaimed. 'You're back early. I didn't hear the car.'

'No, it broke down just outside the village. I walked across the fields.'

'This is Fanny Tarrant.'

'I thought it might be,' Eleanor said.

'Hello,' said Fanny. Eleanor ignored her.

'We've just had a sauna,' said Adrian.

'How nice,' said Eleanor coldly.

'What's the matter with the car?' Adrian said.

'I don't know,' Eleanor said. 'I think it probably just ran out of petrol.'

Fanny suppressed a smile. Adrian caught her eye and grinned.

'Have I said something funny?' Eleanor asked.

'No, it's just . . . never mind,' said Adrian.

'I'd better get dressed,' said Fanny. 'Excuse me.' She went out through the kitchen door.

'I wasn't expecting you back so soon,' Adrian said to Eleanor.

'Evidently,' she said.

'Ellie! Don't be silly.'

'Rosemary had one of her migraines so I came home early,' said Eleanor. 'What does she look like in the nude?'

'I really couldn't say. It's quite dark in the sauna, as you know.'

'What about in the shower?'

'I didn't take a shower with her. I stayed in the sauna after she'd –' Adrian made an impatient gesture. 'I don't know why I'm playing this silly game. I'm going to get dressed.' He took a few steps towards the kitchen, then seemed to change his mind and strode out into the hall and up the stairs.

Eleanor stood for a moment, gripping the edge of the dining table, frowning in thought. Then she walked slowly round the room, like someone looking for clues. She noticed Fanny's tape recorder on the coffee table, and picked it up, turning it over in her hands, as if wondering what it contained. The little machine had no speaker. She glanced at the hi-fi system on the bookshelves. Its operating lights were still on. Eleanor went over and pressed the Play button on the tape deck. The hiss of a blank tape being played came from the loudspeakers. She pressed the Rewind button for a few seconds, then Stop and Play. Her own voice came from the loudspeakers, followed by those of Adrian and Fanny.

' . . . probably just ran out of petrol . . . Have I said something funny?'

'No, it's just . . . never mind.'

'I'd better get dressed . . . Excuse me.'

Eleanor pressed Rewind for another few seconds. She stopped the tape and pressed Play again.

' . . . a rock musician, covered in tattoos. He kept on at me to have one too, and I was so besotted that I agreed. It's a real bore.

81

Means I can't wear sleeveless dresses in the summer.'

'Oh, I think it's rather charming. It looks as if the butterfly has just alighted on your shoulder.'

Eleanor pulled a face, and stopped the tape. She moved a few paces away from the hi-fi, but turned back for one more go. This time she let the tape rewind for longer before stopping it and pressing Play. She heard Adrian's voice.

'. . . seemed to abolish the jealousy thing, the possessiveness thing, at a stroke. It was the sixties, you know: we thought we were reinventing sexual relationships. So the next night I made myself scarce, and Ellie went to bed with Sam. He and I never discussed it afterwards, and –'

With an abrupt movement, Eleanor pressed the Stop button, cutting off the sound. She began to breathe quickly. She looked shocked, then angry. Nearly a minute passed. Then Adrian appeared at the door to the hall, dressed in different clothes from those he had been wearing earlier. His trousers were tucked into his socks.

'I'll take a can of petrol to the car on the bike and see if it starts,' he said. Eleanor, her back to Adrian, did not reply. 'Where is it exactly?' he said. 'This side of the village?' As Eleanor still didn't reply, he came into the room. 'Ellie?' he said, with a certain impatience.

'How could you?' she said.

'What?'

Eleanor rounded on him. 'Betray me like that.'

'For God's sake, Ellie, it was only a sauna!' he said. 'Nothing happened.'

'I'm not talking about the bloody sauna,' Eleanor said. 'I mean telling her about *me*, about my private life.'

'What d'you mean?' he said, but his face said, '*How do you know?*'

Eleanor pressed the Play button on the tape deck.

'**. . . and we went back to being a chaste, platonic threesome. But of course it wasn't the same. We had eaten the apple, or at least taken a large bite out of it. Eventually Ellie had to choose between us.**'

'Oh shit,' said Adrian.

'**In the novel . . .**'

Adrian switched off the hi-fi. 'That was off the record,' he said.

Eleanor pointed to the hi-fi. 'It's *on* the bloody record!'

'I mean, she switched off her tape recorder for that bit. I forgot mine was still on.'

'I don't care what was on or off,' said Eleanor. 'You told a total stranger something very private about me, about *me*, without my permission.'

'I'm sorry, Ellie. But –'

'It's outrageous. I can hardly believe it.'

'Ellie, listen. I'll tell you what happened. I let something slip out, about our student days, Sam and I meeting you, and she was on to it in a flash –'

'Surprise, surprise!'

'I thought it was best to set her straight, off the record. That way, she can't use any of it.'

'Why would she be interested in anything she can't use?'

'I asked her that,' said Adrian, recovering his poise a little. 'It turns out she's a bit of a fan, actually . . .'

'Oh, how nice! Did she bring a book for you to sign?'

'Well, as it happens, she did,' said Adrian.

'For God's sake! You're as bad as Sam!' said Eleanor. 'You both fall for that female flattery like a baby taking the breast. You turn up your eyes and suck, suck, suck.' Adrian bore this denunciation in silence. 'What else did you tell her "off the record"?' Eleanor said. 'Did you tell her I had an abortion?'

Adrian looked shocked and alarmed. He glanced towards the kitchen door and lowered his voice. 'Of course I didn't,' he hissed. 'Are you mad?'

'No, but I think you are,' said Eleanor. 'Suppose she finds out on her own?'

'She won't. She can't,' said Adrian. 'In any case the whole story of you and me and Sam is ring-fenced. She gave me her word.'

'And you trust her?'

'Yes,' he said. 'I do.'

Fanny came through the kitchen door, dressed and groomed as she had been when she arrived.

'Oh, there you are,' said Adrian. Eleanor turned her back on Fanny and struggled to compose herself. Adrian went towards the hallway. 'I'm just going to put some petrol in the car. This side of the village is it, Ellie?'

'Yes,' said Ellie, without turning round.

'If it starts I can run you to the station,' Adrian said to Fanny.

'Thanks, but you needn't bother,' she said.

'No bother. Back in two ticks.' And before she could stop him, he was out of the room.

'No, please –' Fanny called after him; but either he didn't hear or he didn't want to hear. They heard the front door shut behind him. Fanny sighed. 'Actually

I took the liberty of ringing for a cab from the kitchen,' she said to Eleanor.

Eleanor turned to face her. 'What train are you catching?'

'The first that comes.'

Eleanor glanced at her watch. 'You've just missed one. You'll have to wait for nearly an hour. Unless you take the taxi all the way to Gatwick.'

'Then I'll do that.' A silence followed. 'This is rather awkward,' Fanny said.

'Yes,' said Eleanor.

'I hope you didn't jump to any conclusions . . .'

'What sort of conclusions?'

'We had a sauna, that's all. There was nothing . . . sexual about it.'

'You don't see anything sexual about sitting stark naked in a small wooden box with a strange man?' said Eleanor.

'I felt quite comfortable. There was no touching or anything.'

'He seemed to be touching you when I came in.'

'I was showing him a tattoo I have on my shoulder.'

'I see. Well, it makes a change from etchings, I suppose.'

'Look, I'm sorry. In hindsight it was probably not a good idea, the sauna, but he sort of dared me, and

I never could resist a dare.' Fanny went across to the coffee table and picked up her tape recorder.

'Why did you come here?' Eleanor said.

'To interview your husband.'

'Yes, but why him? He's not a well-known author any more.'

'That was what interested me. I wanted to find out why he stopped writing.'

'And did you?'

'I think so,' said Fanny. 'He told me he didn't have anything left to say that seemed worth the bother of thinking up another story to say it with.'

'Did he, indeed?' said Eleanor.

'Not many writers have such humility.'

Eleanor made a wordless sound whose meaning was obvious. Fanny glanced at her with a sudden flicker of interest. Eleanor, still fizzing with barely suppressed anger, missed this glance.

'You don't agree?' Fanny said.

'I've spent too many hours trying to prop up his self-esteem.'

Unobserved by Eleanor, Fanny switched on her tape recorder, and continued to hold it in her hand. 'Well,' she said chattily, 'Virginia Woolf says somewhere that the worst thing about being a writer is that one is so dependent on praise.'

'It's the worst thing about being married to one, too,' said Eleanor. 'If you don't enthuse about their work they sulk, and if you do they think it doesn't really count.'

'Which it doesn't, of course,' said Fanny, smiling. 'Not like reviews.'

'Adrian got wonderful reviews for his first book,' said Eleanor. 'It was the worst thing that could have happened to him.'

'Why?'

'He kept thinking it would happen again, that royal flush of rave reviews. It didn't, of course. Each novel was a worse ordeal than the one before. The tension in the house was unbearable around publication day. He used to sit on the stairs in the early morning in his pyjamas and dressing gown, waiting for the paper to come through the letterbox. Then as soon as I was up, he'd send me out to get the other papers.'

'Why didn't he get them himself?'

'Because he liked to pretend to other people that he didn't bother reading reviews, that he left all that to me. And, for a while, I did take on the job. I would just give him a vague idea of what they were like – the *Observer* was B+, the *Telegraph* A–, and so on. I didn't tell him about the Cs and Ds. But it was no use, he would get them out of the filing cabinet when I wasn't around, and I could tell from his gloom as he mooched about the house that he'd discovered a bad one.'

'He must have been difficult to live with in those days.'

'*Difficult!* He was bloody impossible. No wonder the boys left home as soon as they could ... Between the agony of composition and the ordeal of publication there was a period of about three months when he was like a normal human being. Then the whole cycle would start again.'

'Why did it stop with *Out of the Depths*?'

'His publishers were very pleased with it, and some idiot there put it into Adrian's head that he was going to win the Booker prize, and God knows what else. Well, when it came out, it got the usual mixed reception – some good reviews, some not so good, a few nasty ones from young smartypants out to make names for themselves – and it wasn't even shortlisted for the Booker. Adrian went into a deep depression – which I had to try and conceal from his publisher, his agent, his friends, and the rest of the world. I just couldn't take it any more.'

'You threatened to leave him?'

'It amounted to that. But he'd decided he couldn't take it any more either. He said he was finished with writing fiction. We sold our London house and moved

down here, to start a different kind of life . . . So . . .
It was a solution, but hardly a heroic one.'

'I'm disappointed, I admit,' said Fanny.

'Why?'

'Well, he *was* a kind of hero to me once.'

Eleanor looked at Fanny uneasily. The doorbell
chimed.

'That's probably my taxi,' said Fanny. She switched
off her tape recorder. Eleanor noticed this with alarm.

'You haven't been taping me, have you?'

'Yes,' said Fanny, snapping open the catches on her
slimline briefcase.

'You didn't ask my permission.'

'What difference does it make?'

'You had no right.'

'You didn't say it was off the record.'

'I know, but . . .' Eleanor faltered.

'But what? Why did you tell me all that stuff?'

'I was upset.'

'You were pissed off with your husband so you
shopped him to me.' Fanny put the tape recorder in
her briefcase and shut it.

'Give me the tape. Or erase the bit with me on it.'

Fanny shook her head. 'Sorry.' The doorchime
sounded again. 'I must go.'

Eleanor moved to intercept her as she made for

the hallway. Fanny stopped and stood to attention, with her briefcase at her side. 'Look, I suppose I wanted you to know the truth,' Eleanor said, 'but I didn't necessarily mean you to publish it.'

'"Necessarily?"' Fanny echoed sardonically.

'Please.'

'You know what I do for a living.'

The two women held each other's gaze for a moment. Then Eleanor said, 'Yes, you destroy people's lives. You flatter them rotten and insinuate yourself into their homes, and lure them into making unguarded remarks and betray their confidence and wreck their self-esteem and ruin their peace of mind. That's what you do for a living.'

The doorchime sounded again.

'Goodbye,' said Fanny, and was gone. A moment later Eleanor heard the front door slam shut. She sat down on a chair at the dining table, and stared into space – or the future. Her anger had evaporated. Her countenance now expressed only remorse and apprehension.

4

About two weeks later, very early in the morning, Eleanor sat in the same chair and almost the same attitude, except that she had on the table in front of her a mug with half an inch of cold tea in the bottom. She was wearing her dressing gown over a nightdress. It was daylight, but overcast, and a humid mist hung over the fields. Through the windows of the cottage the landscape looked monochrome. In the distance a cock crew. Eleanor tensed as she picked up the sound of a vehicle approaching the cottage. It turned slowly into the drive, tyres quietly crunching the gravel. The engine stopped. A car door shut with a gentle clunk. Eleanor darted into the hall and drew back the bolts on the front door. When she opened it, Sam Sharp stood on the threshold.

'God! You of all people,' Eleanor said.

'It's terribly early, I know, but –'

'Come in,' she said, though not in the most welcoming of tones.

She led him into the living room. 'I just flew in

from LA on the red-eye.' he said. He was wearing a crumpled linen suit with a food stain on the lapel, and his face was unshaven. 'Thought I'd collect my pot, if you were up and about. Which you are.'

'You said you were going for a month,' said Eleanor.

'My plans changed. How are you, anyway?' He leaned forward to kiss Eleanor on the cheek, but she turned away and sat down at the dining table.

'I don't want to kiss you, Sam.'

Sam was disconcerted. 'Oh.' He drew the back of a hand across his chin. 'Stubble? Bad breath?'

'I'm angry with you.'

'Why? What have I done?'

'You introduced that poisonous snake Fanny Tarrant into our lives.'

Sam looked surprised. 'You mean she interviewed Adrian?'

'Yes.'

'Why didn't he tell me? Did he write his piece about her?'

'Not as far as I know. But Fanny Tarrant wrote hers about him.'

'Show me,' said Sam.

'I haven't got it. That's why I'm up at this ungodly hour. I'm waiting for the Sunday papers to be delivered.'

93

'How d'you know it'll be in today's paper?'

'It was trailed in last Sunday's: "*Fanny Tarrant Tracks Adrian Ludlow To His Hideaway.*"'

'That sounds all right,' said Sam. 'It might be quite a nice piece.'

'It won't be,' said Eleanor.

'How d'you know?'

'It's a long story. I'll try and make it short. Sit down.'

'Can I have some coffee first?'

'No,' said Eleanor.

'No? As in "no"?'

'Listen, damn you!' said Eleanor.

At last it penetrated Sam's skull that something serious had happened. 'All right, all right,' he said. He sat down submissively.

'Your stupid plot worked, up to a point. Adrian's agent –' She stopped and stared at Sam. 'Where's your toupée?' she said. There was a large bald patch on the crown of his head.

'I binned it,' Sam said, a little sheepishly.

'Why?'

'It was a nuisance in California. It kept coming off in my pool . . . Go on.'

Eleanor told Sam how the interview had been set up, against her own advice, and how she had arranged to be away from home. 'But I came home earlier than expected.' She paused, recalling the moment.

'Don't tell me you found them in bed together?' Sam said.

'Not quite such a cliché as that,' said Eleanor. 'But they had just had a sauna together.'

'A sauna? You mean, in the nude?'

'So I understand.'

'Bloody hell!' said Sam in a tone of wonderment, mingled with envy.

'They were lolling about in bathrobes when I walked in. Hers was fetchingly off the shoulder because she was showing him her tattoo.'

'What kind of tattoo?' said Sam.

'What does it matter?' Eleanor said irritably. 'A butterfly.'

'"Floats like a butterfly, stings like a bee."'

'More like a scorpion. She ought to have a scorpion's tail tattooed on her bum,' Eleanor said. 'Well, I wasn't too enchanted with this little tableau, though I didn't seriously think anything more intimate had occurred –'

'You were very trusting,' said Sam.

'He's a fanatic about the sauna, as you know,' said Eleanor. 'He's always trying to convert people. I really don't think he was trying to seduce her.'

'But perhaps she was trying to seduce him?'

'That did cross my mind. But anyway, while they were getting dressed, I discovered Adrian had been taping the interview.' Eleanor described what she heard Adrian saying to Fanny.

Sam sat up. 'Jesus! Is he out of his mind?'

'He said it was off the record.'

'Oh, off the record,' said Sam, relaxing a little. 'But you don't trust her?'

'No. I don't know. The point is, he had no right to tell her *anything* about me, let alone something as private as that.'

'No of course not, but –'

'For years I put up with coming across bits of my private life in his novels. It's not very pleasant, it's . . . like seeing your old clothes, things you thought you'd thrown away, displayed in a charity shop window. But at least I could tell myself that nobody else would know they were mine, because he changed things and jumbled them up. But *this* was something else . . .'

'I understand why you're mad, Ellie,' said Sam. 'You have every right to be. But really, there's no need to get in a state about today's paper.'

'You don't know what's in it.'

'Even if she's used the story, it's not going to make any waves. So you slept with two boyfriends, one after the other, thirty years ago. So what? Who cares?' Eleanor was silent. 'He didn't tell her anything else, did he?' Sam asked anxiously. 'Nothing about the –'

'No,' said Eleanor.

'Thank Christ for that,' said Sam. 'So you've got nothing to worry about.'

'I haven't finished telling you. While she was waiting for her taxi and Adrian was fetching the car –'

'Where was the car, then?'

'What does it matter where the bloody car was?'

'Sorry,' said Sam. 'If you're a scriptwriter you get in the habit of asking these questions.'

'I ran out of petrol just outside the village. I walked home across the fields. Adrian took a can of petrol to the car. Satisfied?'

'So you surprised them in their bathrobes because they didn't hear the car coming. You see: it all fits together.'

'This isn't one of your scripts, Sam, it's my life.'

'Mine too, by the sound of it,' he said. 'So you were –'

'Ssh!' Eleanor held up her hand.

'What?'

Eleanor went to the window and looked out. 'Nothing. I thought I heard Mr Barnes's van.'

'Who's Mr Barnes?'

'Our newsagent.' She returned to the table and sat down again.

'So you were left alone with Fanny Tarrant?'

'Yes. I was angry, upset. She said Adrian had told her that he gave up writing novels because he'd decided he had nothing new to say. She seemed so pleased with herself at having made this discovery, and so admiring of Adrian, it made me sick. So I blurted out the *real* reason why he stopped writing.'

'Why did he?' said Sam.

'He just couldn't stand being continually reminded that nothing he wrote was as good as his first book.'

'You mean reviews? Adrian always said he never read reviews.'

'A complete lie. Which I connived at. But it wasn't just reviews. Any kind of slight, real or imagined, would send him into despair. When *Out of the Depths* wasn't shortlisted for the Booker he was practically suicidal.'

'I had no idea . . .' said Sam. 'And you told Fanny Tarrant all this?'

'Yes.'

'Off the record?'

'No.'

Sam pulled a face. 'Oh dear.'

'I was angry. I wasn't thinking clearly. I didn't realize

she was taping me until she switched her machine off. When Adrian came back, after she'd gone, I confessed what I'd done.'

'What did he say?'

'He didn't say anything,' said Eleanor. 'He hasn't spoken to me since.'

'About Fanny Tarrant?'

'About anything. He hasn't addressed a single word to me on any subject whatsoever since that day, except when other people are present. Then he chats away, and smiles and laughs and draws me into the conversation as if everything were perfectly normal, but as soon as the other people have gone, whether it's neighbours or the vicar or our cleaning lady, he goes stony silent, ignores what I say, and leaves me little notes.'

Eleanor dug into the pocket of her dressing gown and pulled out a handful of folded and crumpled pieces of paper, which she dropped on the table in front of Sam. He picked up one of them, opened it, and read out: '*I shall require the car tomorrow morning between 11.30 a.m and 1 p.m.*' Sam looked at Eleanor. 'Why d'you put up with this nonsense? Why don't you push off and leave him to stew in his own juice?'

'Because I feel guilty, I suppose. For betraying his secret.'

'You didn't mean to.'

'I did really,' Eleanor said ruefully. 'I just changed my mind, too late.'

'Well, it was his own fault. He provoked you . . . where is he now?'

'Still asleep, I expect. He sleeps in the guest room, goes to bed hours after me and gets up late, so we don't have breakfast at the same time. We don't have any meals together, actually.'

Sam thought for a moment. Then he said, 'Ellie, come home with me. Now. Leave *him* a note. That'll bring him to his senses.'

'No thanks, Sam,' said Eleanor.

'You're letting him treat you as some kind of criminal. It's absurd.'

'I know, but . . .'

'Get dressed, pack a bag, come with me now. While he's still asleep. Just do it.' He jumped to his feet as if to encourage her. 'No strings attached. Unless you want them, of course.'

Eleanor smiled. 'Thanks, Sam, but I can't.'

'Why not?'

'If I left now, I'd never come back. That would be the end.'

'Well, maybe you've come to the end of this marriage,' he said.

'Oh, I don't want a divorce, Sam!' Eleanor exclaimed. 'Everybody I know has been divorced. I've seen what it does to people. *You* know what it's like. I don't want to go through all that, not at my time of life. I should have done it ten years ago, if I was going to do it.'

'But if the marriage has gone sour –'

'No, since we came to live here, things have improved a lot,' said Eleanor. 'Adrian can be lovely when he's in a good mood.'

'Oh, I know that.'

'And since he gave up writing novels he's been in a good mood nearly all the time.' She added, 'Or he's pretended to be, which amounts to the same thing as far as I'm concerned.' The attempt at flippancy was belied by a huskiness in her voice.

'Why did you marry him, Ellie?' Sam said.

Eleanor hesitated for a moment, like someone on a brink. Then she jumped. 'He was the father,' she said.

'What?'

'When I had the abortion.'

Sam stared at her. 'You said you didn't know which of us was the father.'

'But I did know. I was protected when I slept with you.'

'But not when you slept with Adrian?' said Sam. Eleanor nodded. Sam threw his arms into the air. 'Jesus! Why didn't you say at the time?'

'I thought it was the best thing to do,' Eleanor said. 'I thought you would both support me, that it would keep us together as a trio if neither of you knew who was the father. You know, like the blank cartridge in the firing squad.' On reflection, she added, 'Or the opposite.'

'I . . . I . . .' Sam, for once, was speechless.

'I was a very muddled, panic-stricken young woman. I just wanted to be un-pregnant. But later I got very depressed about it. One day – it was when you were in America, on that scholarship – I told Adrian that he was the father. He was stunned at first, like you. But after a little while he asked me to marry him.'

'So that you could have children after all?'

'Yes. But I sometimes wonder if the first pregnancy was a girl. I would have liked a girl.'

'She might have turned out like Fanny Tarrant,' said Sam.

'Don't joke about it, Sam.'

'How should I react, then?' Sam demanded. 'I could be angry, if you like.'

'No, don't be.'

'Jesus, Ellie! You deceived me.'

'I know. It was wrong. I'm sorry.'

'And you let me stay deceived.'

'I was trying to deceive myself, Sam, pretending it never happened.'

'I've made enough real mistakes in my life,' he said feelingly. 'I could've done without my fifty per cent share in that one.'

'I'm sorry, Sam,' Eleanor said again. She went over to him and touched him on the arm. 'Say you forgive me.'

'All right. I forgive you,' he said.

Eleanor kissed him on the cheek and sat down on the *chaise longue*.

'How much longer are you going to put up with Adrian freezing you out?' Sam asked.

'Not much longer. However ghastly Fanny Tarrant's article is, it won't be as bad as waiting for it to appear. I have a feeling that, once we know the worst, the spell will be lifted. Adrian will speak to me again and we'll sort it out.'

'And if you don't?'

'Then I might be glad of your guest room,' she said, with a wan smile.

Sam sat down on the sofa. 'When do your papers usually come?'

'You can never tell. It all depends on whether Mr Barnes delivers them himself in his van, or sends his boy on a bicycle. I thought you were the van.'

'Why don't I drive into the village and get the *Sentinel* now?'

'The shop won't be open yet.'

'There'll be one open somewhere.'

'Not at this hour, on a Sunday. Not for miles.'

They sat in silence for a while. 'It's funny,' said Eleanor, 'this reminds me of those Sunday mornings in London when we used to wait for the papers to be delivered just after publication day. It always gave me a queer sick feeling, because you were in suspense, wondering if the reviews would be good, but rationally you knew the question was already settled – they were already printed and irreversible. Lots of people had already read them. I always hated that feeling. I could empathize with Adrian then.'

'Do you want me to stay till the papers come?' Sam said. 'Or would you prefer to be alone?'

'Stay,' said Eleanor.

'Can I have some coffee, then?'

Eleanor smiled and got to her feet. 'Yes, of course.'

'And I need to wash up, as the Yanks say.'

'Use the loo at the back. Through here.'

Eleanor led Sam into the kitchen. A minute or two later Adrian, wearing a T-shirt and tracksuit trousers, came down the stairs and went along the hall towards the front door. Almost immediately he turned on his heel and entered the living room. He looked around as if in search of something. Eleanor came in from the kitchen with a tray bearing crockery and cutlery. Seeing Adrian, she stopped short.

'If you're looking for the papers, they haven't come yet,' she said.

Adrian ignored her. He went over to the magazine rack near the fireplace and took out an old Sunday supplement. He sat down in an armchair and pretended to read.

Eleanor proceeded to unload her tray at the table. 'I'm making some coffee and toast,' she said. 'Do you want some?' Adrian continued to ignore her. 'Sam's here,' she said. Adrian reacted sharply and stared at her. 'He's in the loo,' she said. Adrian turned back to his magazine. 'I've told him everything,' Eleanor said, 'so you might as well give up this silly game.'

Adrian continued to ignore Eleanor. She banged down the last item from her tray on to the table, and went back into the kitchen. Adrian stopped pretending to read. After a few moments Sam came in from the kitchen.

'Adrian! You're up,' he said, with slightly forced joviality.

Adrian stared at him coldly. 'What are you doing here?'

'I flew in from LA this morning. Dropped in on the off-chance to collect my pot.' He went across to the occasional table on which his vase was displayed and picked it up.

'I thought you were supposed to be away for a month.'

'Change of plan,' said Sam, turning the pot in his hands. 'Lovely glaze,' he commented.

'You mean the studio fired you?'

'No, I fired them,' Sam said. 'In a manner of speaking.' He replaced the vase on the table.

'What manner of speaking?'

'I checked out. I decided I didn't want to become a Hollywood whore. There I was, sitting under a parasol beside my private pool in Beverly Hills, working on the umpteenth draft of a lesbian love scene between Florence Nightingale and a young nurse –'

'Was Florence Nightingale a lesbian?' Adrian interjected.

'She is in this movie,' Sam said. 'Anyway, there I was pegging away on my laptop, when I suddenly thought to myself: what am I doing wasting my time on this crap? I mean, sure I'll make a lot of money out of it, but who knows if it will ever be made, and whether they'll use my lines if it *is* made, and who will care anyway in ten years' time?'

'A kind of road to Damascus experience,' said Adrian.

'That's right,' said Sam. 'I feel born again.'

'And bald again, I notice,' said Adrian.

Sam ignored the quip. 'I realized that I was in danger of becoming a scriptwriting machine.'

Adrian seemed struck by something in this metaphor. 'You mean, by turning out scripts like cars off a production line, you don't give yourself time to take stock of the quality of what you're producing?'

'Yeah, exactly.'

'Well, well,' said Adrian. He seemed impressed at last. 'And what are you going to do about it?'

'Take a sabbatical for a year or two,' Sam said. 'Refuse all new script offers. Do some serious reading and thinking. Maybe write a novel.'

'A novel?'

'Yeah, I've always wanted to try my hand at a novel.'

'It's more difficult than you think,' said Adrian. 'So you won't be offering to adapt *The Hideaway* for the BBC?'

'Er, no, not for the time being,' said Sam. He looked a little abashed. 'Sorry about that. I gather our plot against Fanny Tarrant rather misfired.'

'Yes.'

'Did Peter Reeves at the *Chronicle* get in touch?'

'Yes.'

'Wasn't he interested?'

'Oh yes,' said Adrian, 'but the worst I could discover about Fanny Tarrant was that she went to a convent boarding school, not a comprehensive; that she lives with a man called Creighton; and that she has a butterfly tattooed on her shoulder with the initials of a former rock star on its wings. Not much ammunition for a devastating exposé there, you must admit.'

'But you gave *her* some, I hear,' Sam said.

'Eleanor did.'

'Oh, come on, Adrian, be fair. *You* told Fanny Tarrant about the three of us at university.'

'That was off the record.'

'But why tell her anyway?'

'Damage limitation. She was on the scent . . .'

'And why the sauna?'

Adrian was silent for a moment. 'I don't know,' he said.

'You don't *know*?' Sam repeated.

'It was a spur-of-the-moment idea. I suppose I

thought, if I sprang something totally unexpected on her, she might reveal something unexpected about herself,' he said.

'You really took that reverse-interview idea seriously, didn't you?' said Sam.

'You sound surprised.'

'Well, frankly, I'm amazed that you went through with it. Why didn't you tell me?' Adrian didn't answer. 'As I heard nothing I assumed you'd had second thoughts. I'm sorry you didn't.'

'*You're* sorry?'

'Well, I started the whole thing. I feel responsible.'

'Perhaps you'd like to sort it out, then,' said Adrian. 'Arrange to buy up every edition of today's *Sunday Sentinel* and have them incinerated. Go round the country from door to door buying back the copies already delivered at an irresistible premium. Administer amnesia-inducing drugs to those householders who have already read Fanny Tarrant's article.' He looked at his watch. 'I should get started, if I were you. You haven't got a lot of time.'

'All right, I can't undo the damage that's already been done,' Sam said, 'but perhaps I can help you come to terms with it.'

'I very much doubt it.'

'You can prepare yourself psychologically. Fear is your worst enemy.'

'Did you by any chance go into therapy while you were in California?' said Adrian.

'What's the worst thing Fanny Tarrant can say about you? That you gave up writing because you couldn't bear criticism.'

'Is this supposed to be making me feel better?'

'That's the worst she can say. Can you look it in the eye and accept it?'

'No, since you ask.' Adrian said bitterly. 'No, I can't accept it. I can't bear the thought of half a million people knowing that about me. I can't help my weakness, I'm ashamed of it, but I did manage to keep it to myself for twenty years.'

Eleanor came in from the kitchen with a laden tray and put it down on the dining table.

'Ah, coffee and toast!' Adrian exclaimed, in a completely different tone of voice. 'I expect you've already had a champagne breakfast somewhere over the Irish Sea, Sam, but perhaps you'll partake of our humble fare. Shall we sit up at the table, Ellie?'

'Adrian, if you go on in that plummy mine host manner a minute longer, I swear to God I'll throw this coffee pot at you,' Eleanor said.

'I don't know what you mean, my dear.'

'Sam, leave the room,' said Eleanor.

'What?'

'Just do as I say!' she snapped. 'Go into the hall and wait there.'

'Go!'

'Wait for —?'

'Go!'

Sam went meekly out of the room into the hall, closing the door behind him.

'Either you start speaking to me like a normal human being, or I'm going to leave now, instantly, this minute,' Eleanor said. 'Sam has invited me to stay with him.'

Adrian was silent and did not look at her. After a few moments, Eleanor went towards the door. Her hand was almost on the doorhandle when Adrian spoke, in a low voice.

'All right.'

Eleanor stopped and turned. 'Did you say something?'

'I said "all right".'

'All right what?'

'All right, I'll speak to you like a normal human being. I've spoken.'

Eleanor turned back from the door. 'Do you know, I was actually hoping that you wouldn't,' she said, 'so I could walk out of here with a clear conscience.'

'I'm sorry, Ellie,' Adrian said.

'You've been a real swine these last two weeks.'

'I know.'

'It's not as if I *wanted* to come and live down here, Adrian. I didn't *want* to give up my job at the V and A, I didn't *want* to lose touch with my friends, and give up going to the theatre and galleries and shopping whenever I felt like it. I did it for *your* sake. To give you peace. To keep you sane. And what thanks do I get? You blow it all away, just to gratify your vanity. And when I react, you . . . you . . .' Eleanor sank down on to the nearest chair and sobbed. The door to the hall opened and Sam's concerned face appeared. Adrian went to comfort Eleanor, but Sam got to her first and pushed Adrian out of the way. 'Ellie, what's the matter?' he said, putting his arm round her shoulders.

'What do you think you're doing?' said Adrian.

'Why is she sobbing her heart out?'

'It's none of your business,' said Adrian. He tried to pull Sam away from Eleanor. They wrestled in an undignified fashion for a moment, then separated, glaring at each other.

'You know, sometimes I find it hard to believe we were ever friends,' Sam said.

'Strangely enough, I have the same problem,' Adrian said.

'You've become a pompous, selfish, supercilious prat.'

'And you've turned into a vain, swaggering, unprincipled twerp. Fanny Tarrant had you cold.'

'Well, I'm really looking forward to seeing what she has to say about *you*,' said Sam.

Eleanor began to compose herself as the two men eyeballed each other. She took a tissue from her dressing gown pocket and blew her nose.

'What d'you mean, unprincipled?' Sam demanded.

'You were a promising playwright once. You sold your soul to television for the sake of popular success.'

'I'd rather be a popular success than a high-minded failure. You're afraid I'll write a popular, successful novel now, aren't you?'

'The idea of your writing a novel is so grotesque –'

'Shut up, both of you!' said Eleanor. She held up her hand in a silencing gesture. They obeyed her and heard the sound of a vehicle approaching the cottage. 'I'll open the front door,' said Eleanor. 'It takes for ever to feed the papers through the letter box.' She went into the hall. The two men sat down and waited for her to return.

Sam broke the silence. 'What does she look like in the nude?' he said.

'Oh, for God's sake!'

'No, I'm interested.'

'I didn't particularly notice.'

'Oh come off it, Adrian! Are you telling me you persuaded Fanny Tarrant to take her kit off and you didn't notice the size of her boobs or the shape of her bum? Does she shave her pubic hair?'

Adrian did not answer. He was staring at Fanny Tarrant, who had appeared at the door to the hall and stood on the threshold arrested by the sound of her own name.

'I bet she does,' Sam continued obliviously, leaning back on the *chaise longue*, and closing his eyes. 'I bet Fanny Tarrant shaves her bikini line religiously every Friday night, leaving just a narrow tuft of hair on her pubes, like a vertical moustache. Am I right?'

'Wrong! It's vee-shaped,' said Fanny, advancing into the room, followed by Eleanor.

Sam jumped to his feet. He gaped at Fanny. 'What the fuck are you doing here?' he said.

'I happened to be passing,' said Fanny, 'but I wasn't expecting to meet you, Mr Sharp.' Fanny looked pale and had a slightly wild, distracted air. She was casually dressed in a long-tailed shirt and matching trousers.

Eleanor looked angry and confused. 'Did you invite her here?' she said to Adrian.

'Of course not,' he said.

'Perhaps she left something in the sauna,' Sam said.

'What do you want?' Adrian said to Fanny.

'I presume you've read it – my piece about you?'

'No. Our papers haven't come yet.'

'Oh.' Fanny looked put out. 'Well, I shouldn't bother, if I were you. It's not very nice. The thing is, nobody will take any notice of it.' She looked longingly at the table. 'Is that coffee, by any chance?'

'What's this all about?' Eleanor said. 'You're not welcome here.'

'To put it mildly,' said Sam.

'I'm dying for a cup of coffee,' Fanny said.

'Take some, then,' said Eleanor, 'but don't expect me to pour it for you.'

Fanny went eagerly to the table and poured herself a cup of coffee.

'What have you written about Adrian?' said Eleanor.

'Can't you guess? My teenage idol who turned out to have feet of clay. The man who would make his family's life a misery because of a bad review. The writer who had to get out of the kitchen because he couldn't stand the heat, but pretended he'd lost interest in cooking.' Adrian stiffened as he listened to this. Fanny drank the coffee and sighed with relief. 'God, I needed that.'

'Is that all?' Eleanor asked.

Fanny looked surprised. 'Isn't that enough for you?'

'There's … nothing about us when we were students?'

'That was off the record. Could I possibly have some toast?'

Eleanor shrugged bemusedly. 'Help yourself.'

'Can we get you anything else?' Sam inquired sarcastically. 'How about some eggs? D'you like them sunny side up or easy over?'

'No, this is fine,' said Fanny, tucking into the toast. 'I think my blood-sugar level must be low. I was feeling faint in the car.'

'Look, speaking for myself I'm getting tired of this game,' Sam said. 'Say what you want to say and then fuck off. Or just fuck off.'

Fanny looked at each of them in turn, then at the TV set, silent in its corner. 'You haven't heard yet, have you?' she said.

'Heard what?' said Eleanor.

'It's strange, it's as if I'm looking at you through a

glass wall. You're in a different time zone. You don't know.'

'We don't know what?' said Adrian.

About an hour and a half earlier Fanny Tarrant had been sitting in the front passenger seat of a red BMW 318i saloon driven by her partner, Creighton Dale. They were on their way to Gatwick airport, to catch a holiday charter flight to Turkey. The car cruised along in the middle lane of the London orbital motorway at exactly seventy miles per hour. Creighton, being a lawyer, scrupulously obeyed speed limits. He had a clean driving licence and he intended to keep it that way. Whenever they were in a hurry, Fanny would take the wheel, in case they were caught speeding. But traffic on the M25 was light at this hour on a Sunday morning and they had plenty of time in hand.

They had risen at an early hour in the Clerkenwell loft apartment, roused by two alarm clocks and a British Telecom wake-up call, thrown on their clothes, picked up the bags they had packed the previous evening and stumbled out into the east London dawn, yawning and numbed from their abbreviated sleep. But now their spirits were rising as they contemplated the coming holiday. They made a handsome couple, the blonde, lissom Fanny, and the lean, aquiline-nosed

Creighton, his silky brown hair *en brosse*, and they seemed to know it. A CD was playing quietly on the car's stereo system. It was the work of a Belgian band called Enigma, a mixture of Gregorian chant and electronic dance music that they both liked for its seductive rhythms and mildly sacrilegious flavour.

'Did you pack your camera?' Fanny said.

'Yes, but it hasn't got any film in it,' said Creighton. 'I'll get some at the airport.'

'And I want to pick up a copy of today's paper,' said Fanny.

'I thought you were going to forget newspapers for the next two weeks,' Creighton said.

'It's like the last fag before you give up,' said Fanny.

'What have you got in it?'

'The Diary, and my interview with Adrian Ludlow.'

'Adrian who?'

'Yes,' Fanny sighed, 'I'm afraid that's what a lot of people are going to say when they open the paper: "*Adrian who?*"'

'Why did you do him, then?'

'He wrote a book that meant a lot to me once. *The Hideaway.*'

'I don't know it . . . You haven't done a real star for some time, have you? Are they getting wary of you?'

'Their minders are,' said Fanny. 'PR people demand

approval of interviewers these days, and when they hear my name they say no. My only chance is when I manage to speak directly to the subject. Very few people will turn down a direct invitation to talk about themselves, in my experience. Mind you,' she added, 'I haven't had to take my clothes off before to get a story.'

'Oh, was Ludlow the one with the sauna?'

'Yes.'

'He sounds like a dirty old man to me,' said Creighton.

'No, he was rather sweet,' said Fanny. 'And quite harmless.'

'But you've shafted him, I hope,' said Creighton.

'I do believe you're a little bit jealous,' said Fanny.

'Let's say, suspicious,' said Creighton. 'What was it like, this sauna?'

'Just a wooden shed, quite small, with a stove in one corner. Benches on two levels – room for about three people, four at a pinch. No windows to speak of. There was a dim amber light in the ceiling, so you felt as if you were sitting inside an oven.'

'And you were both naked?'

'I had a towel wrapped round me at first, but I took it off, it was too uncomfortable.'

'And he didn't try anything?'

'No. There was just one moment when he . . .' Fanny's voice trailed away as she recalled the moment.

Creighton took his eye off the road to shoot her a quick sharp glance. 'When he what?'

'He touched me. Not in the sauna – afterwards, when we were resting, in bathrobes. I felt very relaxed, quite at ease. I was showing him my tattoo, and he touched it with his finger. Suddenly the atmosphere was rather charged. I don't know what might have happened if his wife hadn't walked in at that moment.'

'His *wife* walked in? You didn't tell me all this before!'

'Creighton, you know we've hardly exchanged more than two words about anything lately, we've both been so busy. We haven't had sex for ages.'

'I intend to make up for that over the next two weeks,' he said. 'I intend to make you quite sore.' Fanny smiled complacently. 'So what did she say, the wife?'

'Nothing much at first. But when he went out for a few minutes she gave me a rather bitter account of being married to him. It seemed to relieve her feelings.'

'So you *have* shafted him?'

'Yes,' said Fanny, 'I suppose I have.'

'Good girl,' said Creighton. The CD came to an end. 'Put something else on,' he said.

'Let's have the radio,' said Fanny. 'It's coming up to news time.'

'News again,' he said.

Fanny pressed the button on the stereo that was pre-set to BBC Radio 4. A news anchorman was talking to somebody on a telephone line about a car crash. It was a minute or two before they heard the words, 'Paris' and '*paparazzi*' and 'Princess Diana'.

'Diana?' Fanny exclaimed. 'My God, what's she done now?'

The anchorman concluded the telephone conversation and said: '*If you've just joined us, it has been officially confirmed that the Princess of Wales died in hospital in Paris, at four o'clock this morning, following injuries –*'

Fanny gasped and clutched Creighton's arm, causing the car to swerve slightly.

'*Diana dead*? I don't believe it.'

'Ssh!' he said. 'And let go of my arm.'

They listened intently to the summary of the news. 'I don't believe it,' Fanny said. 'Diana *dead*! And Dodi, too.'

'And the driver,' said Creighton. 'It must have been quite a crash.' He eased his foot on the accelerator pedal a degree or two, and the speed of the car dropped to sixty-seven miles per hour.

'I don't believe it,' said Fanny.

'Don't keep saying that,' said Creighton.

'But it's so incredible.'

'Not really,' said Creighton. 'If you think back on how she's been behaving these last few weeks. There was something mad, reckless about it. It was bound to end badly.'

'But what a way to die,' said Fanny.

'Yes, good career move,' said Creighton.

Fanny sniggered, then looked slightly ashamed of herself. 'Creighton! That's sick,' she said.

'True, though,' he said. 'Nobody will dare to criticize her any more.'

Fanny was silent and thoughtful for a few moments. 'Oh shit,' she said.

'What?' said Creighton.

'There's something about Diana in my Diary.'

Creighton took his eye off the road to glance at Fanny. 'What?'

'Something not very complimentary.'

'Well it wouldn't be, would it, if you wrote it?' he said.

'Oh shit,' said Fanny again. 'How's it going to sound when the readers know she's fucking *dead*?'

'I don't suppose you're the only journalist in that position this morning,' said Creighton.

'That doesn't make me feel any better,' said Fanny.

'Only trying to help,' said Creighton. 'Damn!' he exclaimed and struck the steering wheel with his fist in chagrin.

'What's the matter?' said Fanny.

'I missed the turnoff to the M23,' he said. He silenced the radio.

'Don't switch it off!' said Fanny.

'It's distracting,' he said. 'That's why I missed the turnoff.'

'It doesn't matter,' said Fanny. 'You can turn round at the next exit.'

'I know I can,' said Creighton, controlling his irritation with difficulty. 'I just don't like making mistakes. Fortunately we have plenty of time in hand.' He nudged the car back to seventy miles per hour.

A few miles further on they came to an exit where Creighton was able to join the opposite carriageway and return to the interchange with the M23. When they were back on their route, Creighton relaxed perceptibly. 'We've only lost about twenty minutes,' he said.

Fanny, who had been silent and thoughtful again for the last ten of these minutes, switched on the car radio. Creighton looked displeased, but did not intervene. The anchorman was talking to a reporter who was outside the gates of Kensington Palace, where people were already beginning to gather, some bringing bunches of flowers. The reporter was asking them why they had come. A woman said: '*She visited the hospital where my little boy was. He had leukaemia. She held his hand and talked to him. She was a lovely lady.*'

Fanny burst into tears. Creighton looked at her in astonishment. 'What's the matter?' he said, and switched off the radio again.

'I don't know,' she said.

'All right, it's sad, it's a shame, but you didn't know the woman. You didn't even like her.'

'I know,' Fanny said, blowing her nose. 'It's stupid, but I can't help it.'

'Is it your time of the month?'

'Oh, for Christ's sake, Creighton!' Fanny protested. 'Aren't I allowed to have some ordinary human feelings? Does it have to be hormonal?'

'You'll feel better as soon as we get to Turkey,' he said, trying to cheer her up. 'As soon as we're airborne, in fact. A holiday begins with the first complimentary drink from the trolley, I always say.'

Fanny brooded in silence for some moments. Then she said, in a low voice, 'I'm not going.'

'What?'

'I'm not going to Turkey.'

'What are you talking about?'

'You don't seem to realize, Creighton, this is mega. The most famous woman in the world is dead. It's the biggest story since . . . I don't know, the death of Kennedy. The impact is going to be . . . enormous. How will the royal family react? How will the country react? There's going to the mother of all funerals. I can't leave England *now*.'

'You mean – cancel the holiday?'

'Yes.'

'We'll lose all the money.'

'Too bad.'

'But we've been looking forward to this holiday for weeks, months! We're both exhausted. We need this holiday, Fanny!'

'It can wait for a few more weeks.'

'I can't rearrange my work just like that!'

'Well then, you go on your own,' said Fanny.

'On my own?'

'Yes. I won't mind.'

'*You* won't mind,' said Creighton. 'What about me? D'you think I want to spend two weeks in a Turkish resort hotel all on my own?'

'You'll probably meet some nice people,' said Fanny.

'Oh really? People usually go on holiday in couples and families, in case you haven't noticed. They're not looking to cultivate friendships with lonely single men.'

'You never know, you might meet a lonely single woman,' said Fanny, and instantly looked as if she regretted it.

'And you wouldn't mind?'

Fanny avoided his eye, though he kept turning his head to look furiously at her in the course of the conversation. 'Not if you practised safe sex and didn't tell me anything about it,' she said defiantly.

'I don't believe this,' said Creighton. 'You're out of your mind, Fanny. You're jeopardizing our relationship.'

'I'm sorry, Creighton, I just can't contemplate lolling round a swimming pool in Turkey while history is being made here. And reading about it in two-day-old papers. Of course I'd rather you stayed behind with me. But if you must go, go. I won't blame you.'

'All right, I will,' he said.

'All right, do then,' she said.

They completed the journey in grim silence. Creighton drove straight to the Departures terminal, and drew up in front of the glass doors. He got out of the car, leaving the key in the ignition, and opened the boot. Fanny stood beside him as he unloaded his luggage on to the pavement.

'I'm sorry, Creighton,' she said miserably. 'Have a nice time.'

He walked away without a word. The glass doors parted and closed behind him.

Fanny got into the car and adjusted the driver's seat. She started the engine and switched on the radio. '*The royal family have been informed at Balmoral, where they are spending their traditional summer holiday,*' said the newscaster. '*It is understood that Prince Charles has told the young princes of the death of their mother.*' Fanny pulled out from the kerb and across the path of a limousine, whose driver braked sharply and sounded his horn. Fanny accelerated away from the near collision. Distraught, weeping, listening avidly to the radio, she missed the exit from the airport that led to the M23 and found herself instead on a quiet country road. She drove on slowly, peering at the signposts she passed for a clue to her direction.

'What don't we know?' said Adrian.

'Diana's dead,' said Fanny.

'Diana who?'

'Diana Princess of Wales.'

'*What*?' said Eleanor.

'How?' said Adrian.

Fanny told them about the car racing through Paris,

the pursuing *paparazzi*, the tunnel, the concrete column, the lethal crash.

'When is this supposed to have happened?' said Sam.

'Early this morning.'

'You're quite sure? Has it been confirmed?' Adrian said.

'Oh yes,' said Fanny. 'We heard it on the car radio, an hour or more ago.'

'We?'

'Creighton and me. We were on our way to Gatwick.'

Adrian looked towards the window. 'Is Creighton with you, then?'

'No, he went off to Turkey on his own.'

'You cancelled your holiday because of Diana's death?' Adrian said.

'Yes,' said Fanny. 'I may have cancelled my relationship with Creighton too. But I couldn't dream of leaving the country at a moment like this.'

'But why have you come *here*?' said Adrian.

'I've got two pieces in today's *Sentinel*,' said Fanny. 'The interview with you. And a Diary piece. Most of the Diary piece is about Diana.' She paused for a moment, pursing her lips.

'Oh boy,' said Sam quietly.

'When I heard the news my first reaction was stunned disbelief,' Fanny said. 'Then I remembered my Diary piece. I thought of people waking up to the news of Diana's death and then later opening the paper and reading my perky sarcasms about her. I remembered every word. "*She wants to have it both ways, to be the Madonna of the Minefields, nursing limbless toddlers on her knee, and the Playgirl of the Western World, lolling about in Dodi's speedboat in a leopard-skin swimsuit . . .*"'

'Lovely,' said Sam. 'I recognize the style.'

'I'm not the only journalist to have made the point,' said Fanny, 'but it's not something anybody would want to see under their byline this morning. I would've given anything to make it disappear, but it was too late, it was printed in black and white, already on its way to hundreds of thousands of homes, beyond recall . . . On the radio they went over to the gates outside Kensington Palace – there are already people outside, laying flowers by the railings. The reporter spoke to some woman whose little boy had been comforted in hospital by Diana. I burst into tears . . . Creighton thought I had completely lost my marbles . . . We had this huge row about my not going to Turkey . . . He just walked away at the airport, left me with the car. I wasn't really in a fit state to drive – I missed the exit to the motorway and found myself driving along a country road. I decided I was safer staying on it. I was listening to the radio all the time, mainly the same news being repeated over and over. I couldn't stop thinking about my Diary. "*Princess Having-It-Both-Ways*," was the sub-head. I thought to myself, why the fuck shouldn't she have had it both ways? Wouldn't we all like to if we could manage it? I thought, what a bloody mean-spirited thing to say. And then,' Fanny said to Adrian, 'I thought about my piece about you in the same paper ... I started scrolling through *that* in my head, and it seemed pretty mean-spirited too ... Then I saw a road sign to your village ... and I followed it.'

'So what do you want?' said Eleanor. 'Our forgiveness?'

'That would be nice,' Fanny said, as if she hadn't expected it. She looked at Adrian:

Adrian shrugged. 'For what it's worth ...'

'No! Don't let her off, Adrian,' said Sam. 'I'm damned if I'm going to.'

'Oh, I wasn't thinking of you, Mr Sharp,' Fanny said. 'I'm not sure I feel any remorse about *that* piece.'

'Well, that's just as well because I was going to tell you to stick your remorse up your arse,' Sam said. 'I never heard such a lot of self-pitying crap in my life.'

Fanny ignored him. 'Look, you needn't feel too bad about my interview,' she said to Adrian, 'because nobody will read it.'

'What d'you mean?'

'Nobody's going to be reading the Sunday papers today – apart from stuff about Diana. They'll be watching TV, listening to the radio and waiting for tomorrow's papers, with their tongues hanging out. There's only one story anybody's interested in right now, and it isn't my story about you. That's really why I came – to tell you that. Now I'll be off. Thanks for the breakfast.'

Fanny went out of the room. They heard the sound of the front door closing behind her, then her car engine starting. Adrian went to the window and looked out.

Eleanor broke the silence. 'It's unbelievable,' she said.

'Fanny Tarrant's conversion on the road to Gatwick?' Sam said.

'Diana dead,' said Eleanor.

'Oh,' said Sam.

They heard the car's tyres crunching the gravel as it drove away. Adrian turned from the window. 'It's so incredibly poetic, isn't it? Like a Greek tragedy. You don't expect life to imitate art so closely.'

'Poetic?' said Eleanor. 'Being smashed to bits in a car crash?'

'But pursued by *paparazzi* ... The Furies of the media. And killed with her new lover. Love and death. Fearful symmetry.'

'Must you turn everything into literature?' said Eleanor. 'She was a real woman, for God's sake, in the prime of life. And the mother of two boys.'

'I didn't think you had much time for her,' said Adrian.

'Well, I didn't . . . or I thought I didn't,' said Eleanor pensively. 'But when she told us', Eleanor gestured in the direction of the departed Fanny, 'when she said, "Diana is dead", I felt a pang, as if it was someone I knew personally. It's strange.'

'She was a star,' said Sam. 'It's as simple as that.'

'Nothing is as simple as that, Sam.' Eleanor switched on the TV and sat down on the *chaise longue* next to him. It was a fairly old set and took some little time to warm up.

'Because I see the event as a drama doesn't mean I'm not affected by it,' said Adrian. 'In fact, I'm more affected than I would have thought possible. Not as much as Fanny Tarrant, perhaps, but still –'

'Fanny Tarrant! You didn't buy that penitential act,

did you?' said Sam. 'It won't be long before she's back in the denigration business, along with the rest of her tribe.'

As the sound of the TV news coverage became audible, Adrian sat down on the *chaise longue* to watch with the other two. 'I don't know,' he said. 'A death can make a difference. Even the death of someone you never knew, if it's sufficiently . . .'

'Poetic?' said Sam.

'Yes, actually,' said Adrian. *'Arousing pity and fear, whereby to provide an outlet for such emotions.'*

'Good old Aristotle!' said Sam. 'What would we do without him?'

'We pity the victim and fear for ourselves. It can have a powerful effect,' said Adrian.

'Be quiet, for heaven's sake,' said Eleanor, who was sitting between them. 'I can't hear what they're saying.' A representative of some relief agency was discussing the Princess's work for victims of landmines with the anchorman.

'You think we're in for a national catharsis, then?' Sam said to Adrian, leaning back and speaking behind Eleanor's back.

'Conceivably,' said Adrian. On the television they were showing library footage of Diana in a safari suit walking alone along a path marked out through mine-infested scrubland, placing one foot firmly in front of the other, her head held high.

'Well, we shall see . . .' said Sam. 'I think I'll be going, Ellie. Where's my pot?' He stood up and looked round.

'Oh, don't go Sam!' Eleanor said. 'Stay.'

'Well, I don't know . . .'

'Adrian,' Eleanor said.

'What?' said Adrian.

'Tell Sam to stay.'

'Stay,' said Adrian, without taking his eyes from the screen.

'I'm jet-lagged,' Sam said to Eleanor. 'I'll fall asleep.'

'There's a bed in the guest room,' she said.

'I thought Adrian was . . .' Sam looked as if he regretted beginning this sentence, '. . . using it,' he mumbled.

Adrian turned to look at Sam. 'Sit down, Sam,' he said. 'I want you to stay.'

'All right, then.' Sam sat down. Eleanor squeezed his hand. They watched the TV. The film clip about mines ended. The anchorman swung round in his swivel chair and spoke to camera.

'Is he crying?' said Sam incredulously. 'I think he's crying!'

'He is,' said Eleanor.

'That's extraordinary,' said Sam. 'That's really extra-ordinary.'

'You see?' said Adrian.

Now the anchorman was asking a reporter at Kensington Palace if the people laying flowers were showing any hostility to the newspaper photographers present, since it has been reported that *paparazzi* were involved in the fatal car crash. There had been some hostility, the reporter said. A woman had shouted at a photographer, '*Haven't you done enough to her?*'

There was a noise in the hall of the letterbox flap opening and newspapers flopping on to the floor.

'The papers have arrived,' Eleanor said.

'Shall I get them?' said Sam.

'No, leave them,' said Adrian, without taking his eyes from the television.

They went on watching.

Afterword

To develop a stage play into a work of prose fiction is a rather unusual literary project. The transformation of novels into films and television serials is of course very common, and I have had some experience of doing this kind of adaptation myself. The 'novelization' of films and television series is also a recognized if rather despised genre. There are numerous examples of works of prose fiction being adapted for the stage (though seldom by the original authors). But moving a story from the stage to the page is probably the rarest kind of adaptation. It may therefore be of some interest to explain how and why I did this to *Home Truths*.

Most of the ideas I get for fictional writing seem to invite the expansive and complex development that is possible in a novel. I wrote my first play, *The Writing Game*, because its basic story-stuff, concerning five people involved in a short residential course in Creative Writing, seemed to have the 'unities' of time, place and action which classical dramaturgy pre-

Helping to put on this play at the Birmingham ... in May 1990 was a hugely exciting, and mostly enjoyable, experience. *The Writing Game* had two subsequent productions, and came tantalizingly close to being produced in London and New York. I was sufficiently encouraged to try writing another play (indeed, I projected a trilogy of plays about the literary life in contemporary society). Again the kernel subject was, I thought, inherently dramatic: the celebrity interview.

As a journalistic genre, the interview goes back to the nineteenth century, when it was imported into Britain from America, but it has enormously expanded its coverage and column inches in recent times. When I began writing novels in the late 1950s, literary novelists were seldom interviewed unless they were very famous indeed, and nobody showed any interest in interviewing me until about 1980. Nowadays the interview – not only in newspapers and magazines, but also on radio, TV and even the Internet – is a routine part of the promotion of almost any kind of artistic production.

The relationship between interviewer and interviewee has also changed over the same period. What used to be a rather bland and deferential conversation has become more probing and more aggressive. Interviewers want blood – the blood of new and personal revelations – in exchange for the free publicity they offer their subjects. They want to assert their own personalities, and to demonstrate their own literary skills. They can become minor celebrities themselves in consequence. The interviewees, on the other hand, are apt to feel wounded and betrayed by such treatment.

The journalistic interview, it seemed to me, was perfect material for drama. It can be a struggle, a transaction, a confession, a seduction, or all these things in turn. In my play, I raised the stakes by contriving that in its central scene the interviewer is unknowingly being interviewed by the interviewee, who is risking his own jealously guarded privacy in the process. Writing (and frequently re-writing) the play was mainly a matter of embedding this action in a context of human relationships, and then finding a dramatic resolution of the issues it raised. It was not until the play had been accepted for production, and the scheduled start of rehearsals was only two months off, that I found a denouement that satisfied me.

The play that was presented in Birmingham in February 1998 seemed to please its audiences, but not enough of the national newspaper critics to ensure a transfer to London, or to encourage a new production elsewhere. About seven-and-a-half thousand people saw the play in Birmingham. I prepared the playtext for publication by Secker & Warburg with no expectation that this would bring it to the attention of many more thousands. Printed plays, even by established playwrights, do not sell in large quantities. From time to time the thought crossed my mind that I might try re-writing my play as a work of prose fiction one day.

When the publication of the playtext was announced, a surprising number of people in the media and the book world assumed that it was a new novel based on my play, and seemed to lose interest when they discovered that it wasn't. This made me think harder about the possibility of turning *Home Truths* into a novella, in which form it could reach a different and far larger audience – not only in Britain but also other countries, where there was little chance that the play would ever be either performed or published. I did not act, however, until I happened to go to Paris, in March 1999, to attend a colloquium on translation. I was met at the airport by my French publisher, who had just read the play, and her first words to me were that she loved it and wanted to publish it. When I mentioned my idea of a novella version, she was even more enthusiastic. I decided that if I was ever going to write it, now was the time, and, as soon as I got back home, I put other projects aside and set to work.

I had always envisaged the new *Home Truths* as a novella rather than a novel, a short book that would retain the dramatic structure and texture of the original play. One reason, perhaps, why the adaptation of plays into prose fiction is comparatively rare is that the average play would have to be considerably expanded to reach the length of the average novel – but such expansion risks destroying the essential quality of the original, its dramatic concentration on a few decisive moments in the lives of the characters. To 'open out' my play to include leisurely descriptions of the characters' past lives, or detailed representation of their thought processes, in a typically novelistic way, would be, it seemed to me, a serious mistake. The only significant addition I made was in the fourth and final chapter, where the greater flexibility of the narrative form allowed me to present the change in my interviewer-character's feelings in more depth and detail than the constraints of a well-made play per-mitted.

Otherwise, the story unfolds in the novella, as in the original play, through dialogue and interaction between the four main characters, on three occasions over a period of three weeks. There is no privileged insight into what the characters are thinking to themselves, or limitation of the narrative perspective to one character's point of view. This is not, of course, a new fictional technique. It was used, with varying degrees of rigour, by a number of English novelists earlier in the twentieth century who were reacting against the literary novel of consciousness, *e.g.*, Evelyn Waugh, Christopher Isherwood and Henry Green. Later Malcolm Bradbury used it to great effect in *The History Man*. But it was the first time I had written an entire story in this mode, and also my first novella.

Whether it 'works' the reader must judge; but I found the exercise interesting and rewarding, and in carrying it out I benefited greatly from the discussions and revisions of the play that had taken place in the rehearsal period, and from my memories of watching it performed on numerous occasions. It is an interesting fact that all modifications of a play that are made in rehearsal become the intellectual property of the author, whatever their source. At least one joke in the text should really be credited to Brian Protheroe, who played the part of Adrian, and there are nuances of expression and gesture throughout which have been carried over from the production to the novella. But there were also several lines and passages which were cut from the play at various stages of its develop-ment either because there wasn't room for them or because they presented problems in performance, but which seemed to be helpful in the novella. Most of the extracts from Fanny Tarrant's hostile profile of Sam Sharp, for instance, come into this category. Finding a use for such work was one of the unexpected pleasures of writing the novella; for like (I believe) most writers, I hate to waste anything that has cost me some effort.

David Lodge